JO IN THE MIDDLE

'They all know each other,' hissed Matty.

'They can't *all*,' said Jo. She and Matty couldn't be the only ones who were new. Matty's fingers curled urgently over her wrist.

'We'll stick together, won't we, Jam? You and me . . . we'll stick together?'

'Course we will,' said Jo.

She and Matty walked through the gates.

Jo in the Middle

Jean Ure

RED FOX

A Red Fox Book
Published by Random House Children's Books
20 Vauxhall Bridge Road, London SW1V 2SA

A division of the Random House Group
London Melbourne Sydney Auckland
Johannesburg and agencies throughout the world

First published by Hutchinson Children's Books 1990

Red Fox edition 1992

Printed and bound in Great Britain by
Cox & Wyman Ltd, Reading, Berkshire

ISBN 0 09 997730 3

To Jenny, who patiently answered lots of silly questions and made a wooden beetle

1

'Now, are you two girls quite sure about this?' said Mrs Jameson. 'You really don't want me to come any further with you?'

There was a moment's hesitation. Jo looked at Matty, Matty looked at Jo. One black face, one pink face (covered, that one, in freckles) both earnestly scrubbed and shining. Uncommonly neat they were, in their new school uniforms – the pleated navy skirts, white blouses, red sweaters and smart navy jackets of Peter High. The jackets had the letters *P S M H S G* embroidered in scarlet on the pocket. The letters stood for Petersham & St Mary's High School for Girls, but that was too much of a mouthful. Most people shortened it to Peter's.

'Don't be afraid to say,' said Mrs Jameson. 'There's nothing to be ashamed of.'

But there was, thought Jo. You couldn't turn up on your very first day clutching your mother's hand; it would create quite the wrong impression.

'You never took Tom,' she said. Tom wouldn't have been seen dead clutching his mother's hand.

'It was rather different for Tom.'

'Just 'cause he's a *boy*.'

'Nothing to do with him being a boy! He happened to be going where all his friends were going. You and Matty are on your own.'

Not completely on their own. Jo pushed determinedly

at the thick fringe of hair which flopped into her eyes. They had each other; you couldn't call that being on your own.

'It's all right,' she said. 'We'll be OK.'

'How about Matty? What does she feel?'

Matty glanced beseechingly at Jo: Jo pretended not to notice. She was the bolder of the two, it was up to her to make a stand. Left to herself Matty would almost certainly give way. She would bring shame upon them both by allowing Mrs Jameson to accompany them right up to the very gates – maybe even up to the very *door*. Jo wasn't having that. Start as you mean to go on, Miss Drew at Juniors used to say.

'We've got each other,' she said. She looked pointedly at Matty as she said it. 'It's not like if there was just one of us.'

'Right.' Matty nodded, nervously determined, her long, black corkscrew curls, which she wore in two bunches on either side of her head, bobbing and bouncing as she did so. 'We've got each other.'

Jo Jameson and Matty McShane had been friends since Matty had come to live next door at the age of nine, and Jo had been deputed to look after her on her first day at Juniors. She could usually be relied upon to do whatever Jo decided. Not that Jo was a bully, just that she tended to be the one who took the lead.

'All right, then, off you go!' Mrs Jameson gave them both a little push. 'If you insist on being independent . . . have a good day!'

Jo and Matty set off together down the road which led to Peter's. Shapcott Road was a long road, broad and leafy, with big old houses standing back on either side. Some of the houses had been turned into offices or doctors' surgeries, some into flats, others into private schools, such as Linden House Preparatory and Beechwood Grove. Peter's had been private but that had been years ago, when Mrs Jameson was a girl. It was comprehensive now, though still single sex. Jo and Matty's mothers had been pleased about that: they said that girls did better on their own. Jo hadn't yet made up her mind; she thought it was something you probably couldn't tell until you'd tried it. At least it would make a change. Tom and Andy, her brothers, and Matty's brother, Miles, jeered and said, 'You're just scared of the competition!' but it wasn't that at all. All she meant was that she'd spent the whole of her time at Juniors in the company of boys and it would make a nice change not to have them there.

'All kicking and shoving at you,' grumbled Matty.

'All loud and noisy.'

'Pushing you around.'

'*Bellowing*.'

'Being stupid.'

'Showing off.'

'Do just as well without them.'

'Ya! Women's lib!' scoffed Tom.

There was no denying that boys could be very tiresome.

'I think it might turn out to be quite fun,' said Jo, as she and Matty stood waiting by the crossing for the lights to change.

'Be more fun,' said Matty, 'if it was all of us.'

By 'all of us' Matty meant all their gang from Juniors, but Trish and Laura and the rest were transferring to Fallowfield: Jo and Matty were the only two who had fallen outside the catchment area.

3

'At least we're together,' said Jo. 'Wouldn't be any fun at all if it was only one of us.'

Jo always believed in looking on the bright side when she could. Matty tended to be rather easily downcast.

All along the length of Shapcott Road were little groups of girls in their red and navy uniforms converging upon the wrought iron gates of Peter's. Even Jo's resolute footsteps began to falter slightly as she and Matty drew near.

'It's *big*,' whispered Matty.

'Not as big as Fallowfield . . . Fallowfield's *huge*. Got over a thousand pupils at Fallowfield.' Peter's only had five hundred. That was another reason their mothers had been pleased.

'You two girls,' had said Mrs McShane, 'you don't know how lucky you are . . . privileged, that's what you are!'

For all her resilience, Jo would have to admit that just at that moment she wasn't feeling either lucky or privileged. She was feeling rather small and new and apprehensive. Fallowfield might have a thousand pupils but at least they would have started off by knowing some of them. Here at Petersham & St Mary's they didn't know anyone. Most of the first years would have come up together from the junior department, which meant that Jo and Matty would be total outsiders.

A surge of navy-skirted figures pushed past them; girls of their own age, shrieking and calling out. Jo heard the name 'Bozzy', and another which sounded like 'Fij'. A skinny black girl with a small, vivid face and hair done into hundreds of plaits shot past them like something fired from a rocket and jumped with blood-curdling screech on to the back of another girl. Someone yelled, 'Nadge! You nutter!'

4

'They all know each other,' hissed Matty.

'They can't *all*,' said Jo. She and Matty couldn't be the only ones who were new. Matty's fingers curled urgently over her wrist.

'We'll stick together, won't we, Jam? You and me . . . we'll stick together?'

'Course we will,' said Jo.

She and Matty walked through the gates. Jo wondered what they would call her, here at this new school; whether she would be Jammy, shortened to Jam, as she had been at Juniors, or Jo, which was what she was at home. She had had to be Jammy at Juniors to distinguish her from Joanne Walters and Jo-Ann Daly. They had all been in the same class, which had been confusing. The teachers had called them Big Jo, Little Jo, and Jo-in-the-Middle. Jo Jameson had been Jo-in-the-Middle.

'Look,' said Matty. She pointed. On a music stand in the centre of the driveway was propped a large piece of card. On the card, in red lettering, it said, ALL FIRST YEAR PUPILS TO USE MAIN ENTRANCE. Away to her left Jo saw the black girl with the plaits go shrieking off towards a side door, adroitly weaving in and out of the crowd of larger, more senior pupils moving in the same direction. She didn't look old enough to be a second year, but obviously, thought Jo, she must be.

In the front hall a teacher was waiting with a clip board, checking off names. She told Jo and Matty to 'Go and wait in the gym . . . just follow the others up the stairs.'

The gym was full of girls sitting cross-legged on coconut matting – that is, most of the girls were sitting cross-legged on coconut matting. Two spirits more venturesome than the rest were perched astride a vaulting horse, another casually hanging by her arms from the wall bars.

Jo and Matty took their place on a vacant square of matting at the front. They sat without speaking. Even Jo, the chatterbox, found she temporarily had nothing to say, though she turned and gazed out boldly enough across the sea of heads which filled the gym. (Matty, more timid, kept her head bent, facing front.) You could tell which were the people who had come up together by the way they sat in groups, giggling and talking as if they owned the place. Instantly recognizable as New Girls were those little silent islands of isolation dotted about in their midst. There weren't many of them, but at least, thank goodness, there were *some*.

The hubbub of voices died away as the door of the gym opened and the teacher who had been in the front hall came in.

'Margery Laing,' she said, as she mounted a dais at the end of the gym, 'come down off those wall bars . . . and you two!' She waved a hand at the couple sitting together astride the vaulting horse. 'Chloë and Felicity, isn't it? Get yourselves off that thing and come and sit down with everyone else.'

'There isn't any room,' said the girl who had been hanging off the wall bars.

'What do you mean, there isn't any room? Of course there's room! *Make* room. Just go and squash yourselves in somewhere.'

'We'll be *suffocated*.'

'Suffocated, she says! Have you ever heard of the Black Hole of Calcutta? Well, then, don't talk such nonsense! You people over there, move up and give these delicate flowers a bit of breathing space . . . that's better. Right, now, for the benefit of those of you who are new to the school, let me introduce myself. I am Mrs Stanley. I'm responsible for your welfare while you're in your first year. If ever you feel bothered about anything, or there's anything you don't understand, I'm the person you come to. In addition, some of you will actually be blessed with having me as your maths teacher.'

Here Mrs Stanley paused, as if waiting for a reaction. Jo, looking up at her, smiled politely in case it had been a joke. Mrs Stanley returned the smile.

'I'm glad that someone appreciates my sense of humour . . . now, is everybody here?' She glanced at the sheet of paper she was holding and began to run her finger down the list of names. 'Nadia Foster! Where is Nadia Foster? Has anyone s—'

Before she could finish, a door behind her suddenly crashed open and the black girl with the plaits came bounding in. A muted giggle ran through the ranks.

'Nadia,' said Mrs Stanley. 'What happened? You missed the notice?'

Nadia's eyes went big. 'What notice?'

The giggle swelled and was quickly smothered.

'The one three feet high in the main drive!' Mrs Stanley said it crisply. 'I don't know! Miss your own nose, some of you, if it weren't joined to your face. What's the point of our treating you like seniors if you're still going to behave like babies? Notices are there to be noticed . . . especially when they're three feet high! Just *look*, another time. Right! Sit yourself down and pay attention. Those of you who have come up from the Homestead' – the Homestead was the name of the junior department – 'will already know most of the things that

7

I'm about to tell you, but just remember that there are people who have come from other schools to whom it will all be new. So no fidgeting, wriggling, or silly uncontrolled coughing, *if* you please.'

Jo instantly felt an overwhelming urge to clear a tickle in her throat. She thought her lungs might burst from holding her breath, but fortunately she was not the only person in that predicament. Within seconds, dreadful rackings and raspings were coming from every quarter of the room. Mrs Stanley waited patiently.

'When you have quite finished,' she said.

When they had finished, Mrs Stanley began to talk. She told them something of the history of the school – how it had started all the way back in Victorian times as Petersham High and had merged some years later with St Mary's to become Petersham & St Mary's; how, to begin with, the buildings had consisted of just one big house; how the two adjoining houses had been purchased later, at about the time of the first world war, and finally, in the 1950s, a fourth had been acquired.

'So it's all grown up in a rather haphazard fashion . . . it may take you a while before you learn your way around, but I think you'll agree it's a bit more interesting than modern glass and concrete. This gym, for instance, used to be a Victorian drawing room over a hundred years ago. Just imagine . . . a Victorian family sitting where you are now!'

Someone cried, 'Ugh! Ghosts!' and the girl called Nadia obligingly began waving her arms above her head and making hooting noises. Nadia, thought Jo, was obviously a clown; you always got one person who was. At Juniors it had been Trish. She wondered what Trish was doing at this moment – whether she and Laura and the rest, Big Jo and Little Jo and all the others, were sitting round on coconut matting being told the history of Fallowfield. They couldn't be, really, because Fallowfield didn't have any history, it had only been built four years ago. Mrs Stanley was right: old muddly places were far more interesting than new purpose-built boxes. For the first time, Jo began to think there might be positive advantages to falling outside the catchment area.

Then Mrs Stanley said something which made her feel apprehensive all over again: 'Here at Petersham we operate the house system. The way it works, you're split into four different groups. . . .'

Jo's hand crept out across the coconut matting: Matty's crept to meet it. Fingers linked they sat rigid, listening as Mrs Stanley explained.

'The houses are named after four of the school's early headmistresses . . . Miss Nelligan, Miss York, Miss Roper and Miss Sutton. For the first two years all your classes will be arranged on a house basis; after that, there's a fair amount of cross-teaching, but the house will still be your basic unit. So, what I'm going to do is read out the lists, and as you hear your name I want you to come and stand out here at the front and form yourselves into four nice neat lines. We'll start with Nelligan, as Miss Nelligan was the very first head-mistress. Is everyone ready? Everyone listening? Nadia, are you listening? Good! Let's begin, then . . . Naomi Adams—'

A very tall girl with a thatch of strawlike yellow hair stumbled gawkily to her feet and made her way, in obvious embarrassment, to the front. Jo was thankful *she* didn't come right at the beginning of the alphabet.

9

She felt sorry for poor awkward Naomi, stuck out there all by herself.

'Chloë Boswood—'

Chloë was one of the girls who had been sitting astride the vaulting horse. She was short and bouncy, with stubby blonde plaits and rather prominent blue eyes. She positioned herself behind Naomi and instantly began to pull faces at two other girls, further back in the gym. Jo guessed that she was friends with the other two and was hoping they would all be in the same house. She just hoped that she and Matty would be. She couldn't bear to be parted from Matty.

'Laurel Bustamente—'

Laurel Bustamente was pink and plump and rather pretty, though a little bit lumpish. The sort of girl, thought Jo, who would hate having to strip off for gym or go out in the rain for PE. A bit like Big Jo. Big Jo had loathed PE.

'Nadia Foster—' Nadia scrambled to her feet. She stood at the front of the gym clasping her hands above her head in a boxer's gesture of triumph. Jo wondered why. Was it some sort of special honour to be in Miss Nelligan's house?

Mrs Stanley glanced up, sharply. 'No antics, Nadia. Get into line.'

Nadia obediently skipped out of sight behind big Laurel. There, hidden from view, she continued her hand clasping. A girl sitting close to Jo and Matty gave the black power salute, fist clenched, stabbing the air.

'Lee Powell,' said Mrs Stanley, 'stop jerking your arm about. What do you think you are, a glove puppet?'

Lee subsided. The list went on: 'Prunella Frank – Julie-Ann Gillon – Emma Gilmore – Sally Hutchins – Joanne Jameson—'

Jo stood up, her heart hammering. She didn't dare look at Matty.

'Felicity Jarvis – Claire Kramer, Margery Laing—'

Squeals of jubilation as Margery Laing came out to join them. She and the two vaulting girls were obviously a gang. Jo eyed them rather wistfully. She and Matty had been part of a gang, at Juniors: her and Matty, Trish and Laura. She would *die* if she and Matty were separated.

'Matilda McShane,' said Mrs Stanley. Oh, the relief! Matty sprang forward, a big grin splitting her face. 'Melanie Peach, Geraldine Stubbs, Ashley Wilkerson.'

Now that she knew they were going to be together, Jo could relax and pay more attention to the other girls in Miss Nelligan's. Ashley, in spite of what seemed a most romantic name, was disappointingly ordinary-looking: tallish, but not *very* tall: prettyish, but not *very* pretty: fairish, but not *very* fair. The brace on her teeth, decided Jo, was the most obviously interesting thing about her.

Julie-Ann Gillon was a black girl, round-faced and a bit tubby, with her hair pulled on top of her head and tied with a red ribbon. Melanie Peach was . . . *peachy*. Peachy-complexioned and peachy-pretty, with luminous dark eyes and masses of thick chestnut-coloured hair. Jo thought that she would reserve judgement on Melanie Peach.

Of the others, she thought that Geraldine Stubbs looked serious and dependable, if perhaps a little bit stern; that Prunella Frank looked mad and messy, what with her round pink specs and dark spiky hair which stuck out in all directions; and that Sally Hutchins and Emma Gilmore were like little squat bookends. She might almost have thought they were twins if they hadn't had different names.

11

The girl called Claire Kramer was the one she was most fascinated by. She was small and slender, with large grey eyes in a little pointed face, and long blond hair tied back in a pony tail. Jo thought she had never seen anyone so dainty-looking. It made her feel almost clumping by comparison.

There were mutterings and groanings as Mrs Stanley worked her way through the other three houses. Lots of people from the Homestead had obviously been split up and weren't very happy about it. Others, like Margery Laing and the vaulting horse couple, had been more lucky. You could tell at a glance who were friends. The bookends were, for instance, and Geraldine Stubbs and Prunella Frank.

When Mrs Stanley had finished and everyone was standing in their four more-or-less straight lines at the front of the gym she told them that '*without undue scuffling and fuss*' they were to range themselves into height order.

Scuffling and fuss immediately ensued. Squabbles broke out. People stood back to back and beseeched their friends to judge – and then instantly disputed the verdict if it went against them.

'I'm at *least* half a centimetre taller than her!'

In the end they sorted themselves out. Naomi Adams was the tallest in Nelligan's, with Felicity Jarvis next and then Matty; one of the bookends was the shortest. Jo came just below the half way mark, between Geraldine Stubbs, who was taller, and Claire Kramer, who was a tiny bit shorter.

Because she was next to Claire, who was so exquisite and so dainty, Jo made a conscious effort to stand as they had been taught by Mrs Guy, their drama teacher at

Juniors: straight-backed and head held high. She still felt clumping, though. Claire was like one of the fragile pieces of porcelain which her dad sometimes had for sale in his antique shop and which Jo and Tom were strictly forbidden to touch, or even just breathe on.

When all the scuffling and shuffling had finally stopped, along with the angry accusations of cheating – 'You stood on your toes!' 'No, I did not!' 'Well, then, you're wearing heels!' 'No, I am *not!*' – Mrs Stanley said that this was the order in which they would come into assembly every morning. (But suppose someone suddenly grew an extra three centimetres overnight? wondered Jo.) During the day, said Mrs Stanley, they would be given their house 'colours' – blue for Nelligan, yellow for York, green for Sutton and red for Roper – which in winter they were to wear pinned on to their ties, above the V of their sweaters, and in summer on to the collars of their dresses.

'That way we can all see at a glance which house anyone is in.'

A voice from somewhere further down the line from Jo spoke out, cheekily: 'So you can know who to give order marks to!'

Mrs Stanley didn't seem to mind the interruption. She said: 'All I can say, Nadia, is if the cap fits . . . some people do have rather a habit of collecting order marks, don't they?'

Lots of people from the Homestead laughed at this. Claire Kramer didn't laugh, so maybe she was new; on the other hand, Geraldine Stubbs didn't laugh, either, and Jo was almost certain that she had come up from the Homestead. Geraldine turned and frowned rather dreadfully in the direction of Nadia: order marks, decided Jo, were obviously not a good thing.

Mrs Stanley said that '*keeping in line*' they were to follow her and she would take them to their classrooms. Silently, in single file – Nelligan, followed by York, followed by Sutton, followed by Roper – they set off after Mrs Stanley. As they reached the doors, Matty risked a quick turn of the head and mouthed something at Jo, further down the line. Jo couldn't read what Matty was trying to say, but she didn't need to. Matty was reminding her of their agreement – 'We'll stick together, won't we?'

Of course they would! thought Jo.

2

At Juniors, during their last year, Jo and Matty had always shared a table with Trish and Laura. Here at Peter's they didn't have tables but individual desks, arranged in pairs in three rows across the room, and their form mistress, Miss Lloyd (who had lovely long blonde hair and smelt deliciously of perfume but at the same time looked as if she could be rather strict) said that for the first term they were to sit themselves in alphabetical order.

'I know some of you already have your own particular friends, but some of you haven't. I want those who are new to have a chance to find their feet; I don't want them all herded together in a corner and ignored.'

The only two people who seemed at all pleased with the resulting arrangement were the bookends, Emma Gilmore and Sally Hutchins, who ended up together. Jo found herself sitting in the middle of the class, sharing desks with Felicity Jarvis, a rather thin, wispy girl with droopy mouse-coloured hair and a face like the Virgin Mary in a painting which had hung over the piano at Juniors: long and pale without any eyebrows.

In the desk behind were Laurel Bustamente, all plump and pink, and little Nadia Foster, with her vivid spider monkey face and hundreds of plaits. (Matty had tried doing her hair like that once but had lost patience half way through.) In the desk in front were the forbidding Geraldine Stubbs and the nondescript Ashley. Matty was miles away, over by the windows next to glamorous Melanie.

'Now, we shall vote for form prefects,' said Miss Lloyd, 'since we have to have them, and there'll only be a riot if I choose them myself, though strictly speaking it's not fair on the new people. If it's any consolation, you'll get the chance to put things right next term. If this lot displease you, you can chuck them out. So, let's start with nominations . . . who wants to nominate someone for form captain?'

Three people were nominated: Geraldine Stubbs, Margery Laing and Felicity Jarvis. Miss Lloyd wrote their names on the board, then said that each nominee must stand up and let the new people see who they were, so they could decide who they wanted to vote for.

Jo, who on the whole was a conscientious girl, studied each candidate very earnestly before making up her mind to vote for Felicity. Margery Laing, who had hung off the parallel bars, was a big square sort of girl with a big square sort of face framed with curly dark hair. She was good-looking in a rather boyish way, and Jo thought perhaps she might be a bit bossy, like one of the Jos at Juniors had been. *She* had had a square sort of face.

Geraldine Stubbs might also be bossy, and she couldn't help remembering the stern frown she had directed at Nadia on the subject of order marks. Felicity, she thought, looked far more approachable. Just before Miss Lloyd asked for a show of hands, Felicity leaned in to Jo and whispered: 'It's all right, I'll close my eyes when it's my turn . . . that way I won't know who you've voted for.'

Jo thought that was most considerate. She *might* have

felt a bit awkward, sharing a desk with Felicity and voting for one of the others. If she had wanted to vote for one of the others, that is.

Miss Lloyd wrote the results on the board. They were:

Geraldine Stubbs	8
Margery Laing	5
Felicity Jarvis	2

which meant that Geraldine was captain and Margery vice captain. Felicity whispered, 'Gerry always gets in.' She didn't sound at all put out about it; it was obviously what everyone from the Homestead had expected.

After form captain, they had to vote for games. Felicity was nominated a second time, along with Nadia Foster and Chloë Boswood. Jo thought that she would vote for Felicity again, on the grounds that Nadia was obviously what her mum would have called 'a trouble pot' and Chloë, with her stubby plaits and her big blue bulgy eyes, looked far too childish to be captain of anything. She looked as if she ought still to be in juniors.

This time, the vote was even more decisive:

Nadia Foster	10
Felicity Jarvis	3
Chloë Boswood	2

Nadia must either be extremely good at games, thought Jo, or extremely popular; or maybe both at the same time. At any rate, she was glad that Felicity was vice captain.

After voting, they were given printed timetables to fill in. Jo had been secretly longing for a timetable ever since Tom had come home from his first day at senior school with a sheet of paper covered in what at that time had looked to Jo like Egyptian hieroglyphics or some kind of secret code.

'What's *HUM*?' she'd said.

'Hum is humanities,' had said Tom, all self-important.

'What's CDT?'

'Craft Design and Technology. Nothing you'd understand.'

Now she was filling in her own sheet of paper with the same code – CDT and PSE and HUM, not to mention lots and lots (she was glad to note) of PE.

At break Miss Lloyd said that none of the new girls was to be allowed to go off by herself – 'I want you lot from the Homestead to remember your manners and show people where things are.' By now Jo had worked out who the other new girls were. Apart from Matty and herself there was Claire Kramer, Naomi Adams and Melanie Peach. Felicity said: 'Do you want me to show you where you can buy buns and things?'

Jo beamed and nodded. 'Yes, please!' she said. She looked round for Matty.

'Hey! Jam!' Matty was shouting to her from the door. She was with the black girl, Julie-Ann.

'Is that your friend?' said Felicity. 'That's all right, then . . . looks as if Jool's going to take care of you.'

Felicity raced off after her own friends, leaving Jo to join Matty and Julie-Ann. Jo felt just the tiniest bit regretful: she had already decided that she liked Felicity, with her long droopy hair and pale Virgin Mary face.

Julie-Ann said, 'Were you two at the same school? Is that how you know each other?'

'Yes,' said Matty.

'*And* we live next door,' said Jo.

'Oh.' Was it her imagination, or did Julie-Ann's face fall slightly?

18

'We've been friends for years,' she said. 'Haven't we, Mat?'

'Years and *years*,' said Matty.

They linked arms, so that Julie-Ann was forced to walk ahead. It gave Jo a small feeling of satisfaction. It wasn't that she had anything against Julie-Ann, but Matty was *her* friend and they had vowed to stick together.

Julie-Ann said that they would go to the refectory first, because you could buy buns in the refectory – 'Ones with currants and pink icing' – and after that she would take them down and show them the notice board.

'What notice board?' said Jo, as she picked currants out of her bun.

'House notice board. It tells you what's happening. And if you don't want your currants,' said Julie-Ann, 'can I have them?'

Jo frowned. Traditionally, Matty always ate any food that Jo didn't like. (Food that Jo didn't like included currants, custard, rice pudding, tomatoes, cauliflower, cabbage, candied peel, stewed apples, tinned pears, vanilla ice cream, chocolate ice cream, hazelnut ice cream, marzipan, milk, fried eggs and peanut butter. Fortunately Matty liked all of those things except rice pudding.)

'It's all right,' said Matty. 'She can have them.'

Grudgingly, Jo handed them over. If you asked her, Julie-Ann was already quite tubby enough without eating other people's currants that they didn't want.

'Are you going to join things?' said Julie-Ann.

'What things?'

'Clubs and things. It tells you on the notice board. We have to look at the notice board,' said Julie-Ann, happily munching currants, 'every week to see what's happening . . . like in case there's house meetings or team practices.'

'Games teams?' said Jo.

'Netball and stuff. Everbody has to go to house meetings but you only have to go to team practices if you're in a team. It's for PE freaks, mostly.'

'Jam's a PE freak,' said Matty.

'No, I'm not,' said Jo; but she couldn't help adding, trying not to sound too eager in case anyone thought it really mattered, 'What do you have to do to get into a team?'

'They have these trials,' said Julie-Ann.

'You mean like sheepdog trials?' said Matty. She giggled, and so did Julie-Ann. Jo, rather crossly, swallowed the last of her bun as Julie-Ann led the way back out of the refectory.

'When we were at Juniors,' she said, 'Mat was school champion.'

'That was at running,' said Matty.

'Well, that's PE!'

'Yeah, but it's athletics.'

'Athletics is all right,' said Julie-Ann. 'I don't mind athletics. It's games I can't stand. Netball and rounders and stuff. And *hockey*. Next term we have to play *hockey*.'

Matty rolled her eyes and groaned. Just for a minute, Jo felt like shaking her. It was only on Saturday that she and Matty had had a hockey practice in Jo's back garden with a couple of garden canes and a tennis ball and Matty had agreed with Jo that it seemed like a good game. Now here she was, groaning and pulling silly faces, pretending not to be looking forward to it, just to keep Julie-

20

Ann happy. Unless – a disquieting thought struck her – unless she had been pretending on Saturday just to keep *Jo* happy?

She put the thought from her and did a little hurried skip to catch up. She couldn't link arms again with Matty because there wasn't room for three abreast. Jo skulked behind, trying to overhear what the other two were talking about. It didn't sound particularly enthralling; only some grumble of Julie-Ann's about people that had been together in the Homestead being split up and put in other houses and how her best friend was now in Roper's and *all* of Nadge's friends had been taken away from her and it really wasn't fair, did Matty think it was fair? Matty agreed that it wasn't, but Jo thought they must have had their reasons. They wouldn't do things for no reason at all; at least, she couldn't imagine that they would. There wouldn't be any point.

They reached the notice board and Julie-Ann said, 'It's good coming now 'cause it's not crowded.' As an afterthought she added: 'We're not supposed to be indoors at breaktime.'

Jo was alarmed. 'Hadn't we better go outside, then?'

'It's all right,' said Julie-Ann. 'I don't expect they'll mind, first day of term. What clubs are you going to join?'

There were clubs of all kinds – drama, chess, photography: sketching, Christian Union, rambling: music, stamp collecting, correspondence . . .

'What's correspondence?' said Jo.

'Writing letters.' Julie-Ann sounded surprised that anyone could be so ignorant.

'Writing letters to *who*?' said Jo.

'Pen pals. You can put your name down for two in your first term, then—'

'Two pen pals?'

'Two *clubs*. Then after—'

'Do they arrange for them?'

Jo had often thought she would like to write to someone in a foreign country. Someone in Japan, or Africa – somewhere a long way away. Russia, maybe. She wondered if they let you have pen pals in Russia.

'Do they get them for you?' she said.

Julie-Ann didn't answer her: she and Matty were too busy giggling. What were they giggling about? Jo turned away, rather haughtily. She would join the drama club, she decided, and the correspondence club. And she would put her name down for the Under-13s netball trials. She opened her bag and felt round for her pen.

'So what are you joining?' said Matty.

She should have said, what are *we* joining. Jo and Matty always did things together.

'Drama?' said Jo. 'And correspondence?' She never laid down the law, that would come under the heading of bossiness. You had to be prepared for discussion. But the fact was that Matty nearly always ended up doing what Jo suggested. Jo's pen hovered over the sheet of paper with the words DRAMA SOCIETY at the top of it. 'Shall we?'

'You can,' said Matty. 'I'm going to join the photography club.'

'*Photography*?' Since when had Matty been interested in photography? 'What d'you want to join that for?'

'Fancy it,' said Matty.

'But you haven't got a camera!'

'Get one for my birthday,' said Matty. She sounded very definite about it, as if she had made up her mind that that was what she was going to do whether Jo liked it

22

or not. It wasn't often that Matty made a stand, but when she did she could be stubborn. Jo hesitated. She didn't like the thought of her and Matty doing different things – but Jo wasn't interested in photography. And she wasn't any good at it. Last year on holiday she had used Andy's camera for taking snapshots of the family and all that had come out were odd bits of hands and feet plus half an occasional face. Tom had said she ought to go and have her eyes tested: she obviously needed glasses.

'Know what I'm going to join?' said Julie-Ann. 'I'm going to join the stamp collecting.'

Stamp collecting! That was for kids! Jo had grown out of it years ago. She could hardly believe it when she heard Matty's voice saying that she thought she might join stamp collecting, too.'

'You don't collect stamps!' said Jo.

'I can start,' said Matty. But why would she *want* to? Jo looked at her, reproachfully.

'What about drama?'

'That means doing plays and things,' said Julie-Ann. Well, of course it did! What did she think? People were idiots, or something?

'You could always join the stamp collecting', said Matty.

She didn't want to join the stamp collecting. Jo pushed fretfully at her fringe. Matty wasn't being fair! *She* was the one who'd said stick together. Now she was proposing to go off and do all these stupid things by herself.

'Stamps are fun,' said Julie-Ann. 'You learn things about other countries.'

You'd learn a lot more about other countries, thought Jo, crossly, if you wrote to people that lived in them.

'So are you going to?' said Matty.

23

Jo fought for a moment with her conscience. She *could* offer to join the stamp club if Matty would join drama; but then that would mean not having a pen pal and she wanted a pen pal.

'What about teams?' she said. 'We could try for the Under-13s netball.'

'I'm going to try for the choir,' said Matty.

There was a pause; awkward, embarrassed.

'Well, I s'pose I *could* try for the netball,' said Matty.

'I s'pose I could have a *go* at the choir,' said Jo.

It still wasn't properly fair: Matty was quite good at netball whereas Jo couldn't sing to save her life. But at least they would be doing something together.

3

'So how is life as a Big Real Schoolgirl?' said Jo's dad, all jovial, at breakfast one morning. 'Is it everything you dreamed of?'

'Yes, thank you,' said Jo. She said it in what her mother called her 'prim' voice. What it meant was, I will answer you politely as you are a grown-up, but I consider your attitude to be grossly insulting.

She knew her father couldn't help it; all fathers thought it funny to tease and make silly comments. Matty's did it as well, though not as often as Jo's.

'It's just *men*,' Matty had said once. 'It's sort of programmed into them.'

'Big Real Schoolgirl at a Big Real School,' said Jo's dad.

Jo bent her head over her muesli. It might be programmed into them, but she did think it was about time he had a go at someone else. Tom, for instance; *he* could do with being taken down a peg or two. It wasn't fair, keeping on at Jo. It was years since she'd paraded the house with a Sainsbury's shopping bag full of exercise books declaring herself 'a Big Real Schoolgirl going to a Big Real School.' Not since she was six and a half, in fact, which was when Andy had left Juniors to go to Milden Hall.

'Are they keeping your nose to the grindstone? Given you any homework yet?'

'Yes, thank you,' said Jo. 'Oodles of it.'

'Oodles?' said her dad. 'Oodles and noodles?'

What was funny about *that*? It was just childish. Jo dug her spoon into her muesli.

'Two pages of maths, one page of French, think of something for CDT and an essay to write for English.'

'Cor!' said Andy. He was another who thought it funny. 'A whole essay? That's going it!'

'Why?' Jo looked at him. 'What d'you have?'

'A load more than that,' said Tom, 'I can tell you.'

'You don't have *any* more than that!' Andy might, because of being in his GCSE year, but Tom was hardly any further on than Jo.

'I spent three hours last night,' said Tom, 'just doing theorems.'

If Tom had spent three hours, that was because he was an idiot. Obviously couldn't cope. Rashly, Jo said so. Tom's face grew angry and red.

'You're a fine one to speak! I bet you haven't even *started* theorems . . . bet you don't even know what a theorem *is*!'

'Yes, I do,' said Jo. 'It's geometry.'

'Yeah, and I bet you don't even *do* geometry! Don't expect they'll waste their time trying to teach it to you lot. Not much point at a *girls'* school.'

'Why not?' said Jo's mum. 'I hear that some of you boys are doing needlework these days.'

Jo giggled. Tom spluttered into his muesli and almost choked.

'We are not doing needlework!' A mouthful of muesli shot across the table and splatted on to Jo's plate.

'*Ugh!*' said Jo. 'You're revolting!'

'And you're a grommet!' retorted Tom. A grommet

was one of Tom's made-up words. Nobody knew what it was supposed to mean, but something unpleasant, that was for sure. Tom only made up unpleasant words. 'Look at her!' he said, waving his spoon in derision. 'Wearing a *tie*! What's she think she is? A boy?'

'It's uniform!' cried Jo. She was proud of her school uniform, she wasn't having Tom mock at it.

'Girls don't wear *ties*,' said Tom. 'Not unless they're lesbians.'

'No, and boys don't wear purple,' screeched Jo. 'Not unless they're peculiar!'

Tom's face, at this, turned almost as purple as his school sweater.

'You asked for that,' said Andy.

'At Fallowfield–' Jo stirred carelessly at her muesli. She was glad she had scored over Tom. He deserved it. '– at Fallowfield they wear brown. That's *really* butch.'

'Fallowfield's a heap of sh—' began Tom. His mother intervened just in time.'

'You can stop that!' she said. 'We'll have none of that sort of language, thank you. And as for this sexist nonsense . . . you ought to be ashamed of yourselves.'

'I didn't start it,' said Jo.

The person who had started it – her dad, with his silly jokes about Big Real Schoolgirls – had gone out to the hall to fetch the post. He would probably stay out there, if he thought there was going to be trouble. Jo's mum was always complaining that 'he leaves the telling off to me'.

'You can all get on and finish your breakfast . . . look at the time! You'll be late if you don't hurry.'

Jo wouldn't be late: Peter's was nearer than Milden Hall. She sat, smugly marmalading a slice of toast, while

27

Andy rushed out to the garage for his bicycle and Tom, cramming food into his mouth, stomped noisily upstairs in search of last night's homework. (She just didn't believe it had taken him three hours; not unless he really *was* an idiot.)

The back door slammed: the front door slammed. Jo and her mum were alone in the kitchen.

'So how *is* school?' said her mum. 'Really?'

'It's great,' said Jo. She was into her second week, now, and already the strangeness was beginning to wear off. Of course, she was still a *new* girl (as opposed to those who had come up from the Homestead: the ex-Homesteaders tended to consider themselves something of an elite) but at least she had Matty. It must be horrid, she thought, being new all on your own, like Naomi Adams was, and Claire Kramer.

'Good!' said Mrs Jameson. 'So I take it you've got no problems?'

'Not really,' said Jo.

She only had one problem, and that was Julie-Ann. Julie-Ann lived just a few roads away from Jo and Matty. She caught the same bus home after school, and quite often managed to be on the same bus in the mornings. She was with them every break time. She ate with them in the refectory. In lessons such as art and music, where you could choose your own seats, she sat next to them. Matty didn't seem to mind. It was Jo who minded. Julie-Ann was so *pushy* – she would keep trying to encroach. Sometimes she treated Matty almost as if Matty were her friend rather than Jo's.

For instance, that morning, when 1N (the N stood for Nelligan) had a double period of Home Ec. and Mrs Dyer told them to choose partners, she actually had the nerve to suppose that Matty might be going to partner her. Jo just glared, until in the end Julie-Ann got the message and backed off, but you could tell she was resenting it.

'Who's she think she is?' demanded Jo, beating at her and Matty's rock cake mix with a wooden spoon.

'She's all right,' said Matty. 'She just wants to be friends.'

'I don't mind her being *friends*—' Bash, batter, slosh. That wasn't quite true. She did mind: she was jealous. Jealousy was horrid. She reminded herself that Julie-Ann's best mate had been put into another house, which meant they hardly saw each other. Imagine how it would be if she and Matty had been put in different houses. Cross, because now she had made herself feel mean and petty, she fetched the rock cake mix a resounding *splat* with the wooden spoon: a large gob of goo flew out of the mixing bowl and landed with a flob on the table.

'Now look what you've done!' cried Matty. She grabbed at the bowl. 'Give it me, you're ruining it!'

'So what?' said Jo. 'It's only stupid rock cakes.' Who wanted to learn how to cook rock cakes? Who wanted to learn how to cook *any*thing? Jo didn't like cooking; she didn't see the need for it. If she had her way everyone would exist on nuts and berries, like gorillas. 'Just think,' she said, 'how much work it would save if we ate everything raw.'

'Raw rock cake would be *foul*,' said Matty.

'Be better than cooked rock cake.' Jo dug a finger in the bowl and scooped out a dollop. 'Here!' She thrust her finger at Matty. 'Try some.'

'No!' Matty whacked at her with the spoon. 'Go and grease the baking tin and stop messing around.'

Not surprisingly, Jo and Matty's rock cakes turned out

29

like lumps of concrete. Jo thought it quite funny, especially when Nadia shrieked 'Cannon balls!' and hurled one across the Home Ec. room at Margery Laing. Matty, unusually for her, chose to take offence. She stalked off in a huff and wouldn't talk to Jo for the whole of the rest of the day. Jo was quite put out. Fancy getting uptight about a few mouldy old rock cakes!

One Friday after school the Under-13 netball trials were held. Nadia – or Nadge as everyone called her – had already worked out the form team. It was:

Goal Shooter	. . .	Margery Laing
Goal Attack	. . .	Matty
Wing Attack	. . .	Jo
Centre	. . .	Nadge
Wing Defence	. . .	Sally Hutchins
Goal Defence	. . .	Felicity Jarvis
Goal Keeper	. . .	Chloë Boswood

with Geraldine Stubbs as reserve.

They were all trying for the house team except Geraldine Stubbs, who said that she really didn't have the time. Geraldine was a terribly studious sort of person. She and her best friend, Prunella Frank, always came top of absolutely everything. Sometimes they came top together, and sometimes one of them came top and one of them came second, but neither of them ever came lower than second.

Jo knew this because Julie-Ann had told her. Julie-Ann, having spent five years in the Homestead, knew all there was to know about practically everybody. The bookends, she said, had been best friends since their very first day in the infants. Sally Hutchins, the smaller and slightly squatter of the two, was known as the Mouse. She had been known as Mouse for so long, said

Julie-Ann, that once at someone's party when the person's mother had asked her what her real name was she hadn't been able to remember. Jo wasn't quite sure that she believed this, or at any rate not entirely, but still it was quite funny.

As well as the Bookends there was the Laing Gang. The Laing Gang were Margery Laing, Felicity Jarvis and Chloë Boswood. Margery Laing was known as Barge – 'because she *barges*' – and Felicity Jarvis was Fij, from her initials, Felicity Isobel Jarvis. Chloë Boswood was Bozzy. Up until last term, said Julie-Ann, there had been a fourth member, but she had left to go to another school and now Fat Lollipop was doing her best to move in in place of her. Fat Lollipop was Laurel Bustamente. She *was* a bit on the plump side, but then Julie-Ann herself was hardly what you'd call a stick insect.

There was only one person from the first year who was definitely, beyond any possible shadow of doubt, going to make the house under-13s and that was Nadge. She was the tiniest person on court, apart from Sally Hutchins, but she was also the fastest. Nadge would probably make not only the house team but the school team as well. According to Julie-Ann, Nadge was raving bananas – 'They just can't do anything with her . . . last term she got more than *fifty* order marks.'

It was true that in class there had already been one or two occasions when she was virtually uncontrollable, except by such teachers as Miss Lloyd and Mrs Stanley (they would take no nonsense from anyone) but put her on a netball court and she became a different person. It was almost, thought Jo, watching as Nadge leapt to intercept a ball, as if she had too much energy to be contained within the narrow confines of a classroom.

She was someone who needed to be outdoors, un-fettered.

For her part, Jo would be happy enough just to get into the house team, never mind worrying about the school one. She couldn't decide whether she stood a chance or not. Elizabeth Grey, who was the house games captain – splendid and tall with masses of silvery blond hair – had smiled at her quite kindly as she came off court, but maybe it had only been a smile of consolation? Thank you for trying but I'm afraid it wasn't quite good enough. . . .

'Just have to wait and see,' said Matty, philosophical.

Matty didn't sound as if she specially cared whether she made the team or not. Perhaps it wasn't as important to her as it was to Jo, for Matty had been accepted for the junior choir. Mrs Elliott, the music mistress, had said she had 'very good potential'. She hadn't said that Jo had very good potential. She had demonstrably winced as Jo squawked her way up and down the scale. Afterwards she had told Jo that she thought it was 'very brave of you to have a go. One should always be prepared to have a go. After all, you never know till you've tried, do you?'

The correspondence club had turned out to be a bit of a letdown. Michelle Wandres, the sixth former who was in charge, became quite irritable when Jo said she wanted to write to someone in Russia.

'We haven't *got* anyone in Russia. What would be the point of having someone in Russia? You don't speak Russian, do you?'

'No, but they might speak English,' said Jo.

'There wouldn't be any point them speaking English if you didn't speak Russian.'

Jo found this puzzling. She would have thought there

would have been every point. How else, after all, could you correspond?

'Just look at the list,' said Michelle, 'and choose someone from there.'

Jo looked. 'They're all French and Spanish.'

'Well, what do you expect them to be? Chinese?'

She brightened. '*Could* I write to someone in China?'

'No, you could not!' snapped Michelle. 'Look, just stop wasting my time! Which language are you taking? French, or Spanish?'

'French,' said Jo, resigned.

'Right. So here you are . . .' Michelle pulled out a card and thrust it at her. 'You can go away and write your first letter – *in French*.'

'In *French*?' said Jo.

'Well, of course in French! You didn't think you were going to write in English, did you?'

Jo's cheeks grew crimson. How could she write in French? She'd only had three French lessons. She looked at the card. *Jean-Guy Alain*, it said. *14 rue Tourneur, Paris. 12½ ans.*

'Now what's the matter?' said Michelle.

'Isn't Jean-Guy a boy's name?' stammered Jo.

'So?'

So she didn't want to write to a boy! Specially not in French.

'I hope we're not being *sexist*?' said Michelle.

Matty and Julie-Ann giggled themselves hysterical when they heard.

'It's all right you laughing,' said Jo, 'but I've gone and got stuck with it.'

'We'll help you,' said Matty.

33

'Don't see how you can, seeing's you don't know any more French than I do.'

'Cher Jean-Guy,' said Matty.

'*Yes*?'

'Je suis – what's jam in French?'

'Hang on,' said Julie-Ann. She fished out her French dictionary. 'Con-fi-ture.'

'Je suis confytewer—'

Oh, hilarious! Let's *all* collapse over our desk lids. Jo regarded the two of them, somewhat sourly.

'Fat lot of help you are,' she said.

That evening, assisted by Tom, who had been learning French for two years and had achieved thirty out of a hundred for his last term's French exam, Jo wrote her letter.

Cher Jean-Guy,

Je suis Joanne. Je suis 11½ ans. Je suis à Petersham et St Mary's High Ecole pour Filles. Il est dans Petersham près de Londre. Où êtes vous à école? Mon frère Tom à aidé moi avec ce lettre.

Votre ami de plume

Joanne Jameson.

Tom was especially proud of that last touch – 'ami de plume, that means pen pal.'

Joanne looked at it, doubtfully. 'D'you think he'll understand it?'

'He ought to,' said Tom. 'That's good French, that is.'

She still worried about it. She wasn't sure how much reliance you could place on someone who had only got thirty per cent in his French exam.

4

For gym classes they were divided into three groups: tall, which was Fij and Matty, Naomi Adams, Ashley Wilkerson and Prunella Frank; small, which was Nadge, Bozzy, Emma Gilmore, Claire Kramer and the Mouse; and medium, which was all the rest – Melanie Peach, Laurel Bustamente, Geraldine Stubbs, Jo, Julie-Ann and Margery Laing.

Jo was used by now to being medium; medium height, medium weight, medium clever, medium popular. Sometimes she couldn't help wishing she could be outstanding at something, like Nadge was at games, or Geraldine Stubbs at lessons. She wouldn't even mind if it meant being outstandingly bad at something else by way of compensation. Nadge was outstandingly bad at behaving in class and keeping school rules. Gerry Stubbs, on the other hand, didn't seem to be bad at anything at all, which was just irritating.

Imagine, thought Jo, hanging dreamily upside down from one of the ropes and staring at the gym floor, being such an all-round super genius. All-round mediocrity, that's all *she* was. Jo-in-the-middle – abruptly she reversed her position and went swarming back down the rope – always second fiddle. Hey! she thought. That was a poem! Jo in the middle, always second fiddle. . . .

Lightly, she landed on both feet on the floor.

'Jo!' She became aware that Miss Daley, the gym

mistress, was beckoning her. She ran across. Miss Daley was surrounded by a small group of people – Nadge, Bozzy, the Mouse, Claire Kramer.

'I'm putting you five down for extra gym,' she said. 'I think we might be able to make something of you. Classes every Thursday, straight after school. Start next week. All right?'

Without waiting for a reply, Miss Daley smiled briefly at them and turned to walk away. She had no need to wait for a reply: nobody but nobody would say no to being singled out for extra gym. Jo's spirits soared. Maybe she *wasn't* such a mediocrity after all! Visions of the Olympics rose dizzily before her eyes . . . *Jo Jameson, representing the UK, has just performed a triple back somersault on the parallel bars. . . .*

Suddenly she heard a voice, polite, but in no way apologetic: 'I'm afraid I can't do any extras after school, I have to go to my classes.'

Miss Daley swung back. People nearby, who had been chattering as they did floor exercises on strips of coconut matting, fell silent. Bozzy and the Mouse were both staring, Bozzy's big blue saucer-shaped eyes almost bulging out of her head. Even Nadge seemed somewhat taken aback. Probably no one in the whole history of the school, thought Jo, had ever turned down the opportunity of joining the special gym squad before. (A girl from Petersham really *had* once represented the United Kingdom at the Olympics.)

The polite voice belonged to Claire Kramer. She stood there, before Miss Daley, small but very obviously determined. Miss Daley said, 'What classes are these, Claire?'

'My ballet classes,' said Claire.

'And you say you can't do *any* extras?'

Claire shook her head, so that her blond pony tail swished to and fro.

'So how often do you have these ballet classes?'

'Every day,' said Claire.

'You have a ballet class *every day*?' Miss Daley's voice rose, incredulously.

'Every day except Sundays.'

'Well, in that case,' said Miss Daley, rallying, 'if you have all that number I should hardly have thought it would hurt to miss just one.'

Claire didn't say anything to this. She had her back turned to Jo: it had a stubborn look about it. Jo wondered if her lips were all scrunched up like Matty's when Matty dug her heels in over something.

'Well?' said Miss Daley. There was more than a hint of impatience in her voice. '*Would* it?'

'I'm not allowed to miss classes,' said Claire.

'Oh, now, come! There must be the odd occasion. And in any case,' said Miss Daley, plainly exasperated, 'what do you want all those classes *for*?'

'I'm going to be a dancer,' said Claire.

Something leapt in Jo as she heard Claire say it. How wonderful to be so certain! To be able to state – *I'm going to be a dancer* – with such absolute conviction! Perhaps Miss Daley thought it rather remarkable, as well; or perhaps, as one who was single-minded herself, she was prepared to respect the quality in someone else, even if the thing they were single-minded about was quite different from the thing that she was.

'All right, Claire,' she said. 'I can't argue with that. Mind, I shall expect regular attendance from all of you others. I take it none of you is a budding ballerina?'

37

Slowly, they shook their heads. Everyone was staring at Claire, seeing her in a new light . . . Claire Kramer, budding ballerina . . . hair pulled back into a ballerina's pony tail, feet, even in ordinary gym shoes, managing to look about half the size of anyone else's. Why was it, wondered Jo, that other people, even tiny people like Nadge, seemed so solid and clodhopping beside her? Nadge wasn't solid or clodhopping in the least, she was springy and supple, but in a totally different way from Claire: Nadge looked as if she might have *muscles*. You could imagine her clambering up ropes and doing somersaults and walking on her hands. What you imagined Claire doing were graceful, elegant things in time to music.

Afterwards, in the cloakroom, she heard the Laing Gang discussing it.

'Fancy' – Bozzy's voice was full of scorn and wonderment – 'turning down the chance of extra gym!'

'I suppose there isn't actually a law against it.' That was Fij, always more prepared than the others to be tolerant of humanity's foibles.

'Mightn't be a law against it, but for a stupid thing like *ballet*?'

'I'm not sure one could call ballet stupid, exactly.'

'I could,' said Bozzy. 'I'd call it *dead* stupid . . . people running about on tiptoe all over the place. 'Tisn't natural.'

'Nor is gym, and gym's dangerous . . . people can break their necks doing gym.'

'So they can if they run about on tiptoe! Only got to trip over something.'

'I never actually heard of anyone doing that.'

'You never heard of anyone tripping over something?

Like to know where you've been living all these years!
Obviously not the same place I've been living. Where
I've been living people trip over practically all the time.
Specially if they're running about on their toes. Stands to
reason . . . human beings weren't *made* to run about on
their toes. If God had wanted human beings to run about
on their toes he'd most likely have given them high heels
to do it on. Fact that he didn't,' said Bozzy, 'shows it's
not natural.'

'One wouldn't *mind*—' Barge's voice cut in, heavy
with the weight of authority: Barge could never be kept
out of a conversation for long – 'one wouldn't *mind*,' said
Barge, 'if she'd go and do it somewhere *else* . . . like in a
ballet school or somewhere. What one objects to is
people coming to perfectly ordinary sort of schools such
as Peter's and then behaving in a perfectly *extra*ordinary
sort of way.'

'Like turning down the chance of extra gym.'

'Precisely.'

'I don't see that it should really bother anyone,' said
Fij. 'After all, people don't have to do extra gym if they
don't want to.'

'No, but they ought. If they've been chosen. It'd be
like the Queen offering someone a knighthood and them
saying they don't want it. It's an insult.'

'Yes, it is; it's an insult. *And* she wouldn't be in the
netball team. Nadge asked her, and she said no.'

'Which is more than an insult, it's putting herself
before the team.'

'Except that maybe she has to,' said Fij, 'if she's going
to be a dancer.'

'Well, she shouldn't.' Barge spoke with the definitive
air of one who knows beyond any doubt that she is in the

right. 'People oughtn't to flounce about being different.'

It was at this point that they saw Jo and stopped. Bozzy tossed her plaits and Barge glared defiance; only Fij smiled, slightly awkward, as if they had been caught out in some nefarious act – which in a way they had, all getting together to discuss someone behind her back. And you could hardly, thought Jo, accuse Claire of flouncing. Barge was more likely to flounce than Claire. Clarie just very quietly went her own way. It was that, probably, which had upset them: Barge in particular was dreadfully self-opinionated.

At the end of the third week of term a notice appeared on the house notice board saying that members of the Drama Society were invited to audition for the end-of-term production:

Scenes from *A Midsummer Night's Dream* by William
Shakespeare,
directed by Wendy Armstrong.
Members of the 3rd, 4th, 5th and 6th years to
audition for the following parts:
Helena, Hermia, Lysander, Demetrius,
Oberon, Titania and Bottom
on Tuesday at 4 o'clock in the gym.
Members of the 1st and 2nd years to audition
for the following parts:
Puck, Peaseblossom, Cobweb, Moth, Mustardseed
and attendant fairies
on Wednesday at 3.30 in the small hall.
N.B. *Dancers also urgently required!!!* Anyone
who can dance please write their names below.

Jo wondered whether Claire would put her name down,

or whether dancing in a school production was something else she wasn't allowed to do.

Matty looked at her reproachfully when Jo said she wasn't going straight home after school on Wednesday.

'You're always staying on for something!'

'It's only an audition,' said Jo. 'I don't expect I'll actually get given a part.'

There were a dozen people gathered in the small hall on Wednesday. Others from the first year who were auditioning were the Laing Gang, Laurel Bustamente and Melanie Peach. Melanie Peach turned out to have an uncle who was an actor on television, and thus knew all about auditions. She said, 'The secret is to come prepared; it's no use just turning up and hoping for the best. You have to have done your homework.'

There was a pause; then Barge, belligerent, said, 'What homework? Nobody set any homework.'

'You have to set your own.' Melanie turned her deep, dark, luminous eyes earnestly upon them. 'Like reading the play and knowing what it's about.'

'Some of us already know what *A Midsummer Night's Dream* is about, thank you very much. Some of us don't need to read it.'

'But what about the parts? Have you decided which part you'd be best suited for?'

Someone from the second year, eavesdropping on the conversation, said, 'Bottom!' Bozzy giggled and clamped a hand to her mouth. Barge flushed, angrily.

'It's important,' said Melanie. 'One has to think about these things. I, for instance–' she swished her hair back over her shoulders. It was lovely lush hair, thick and springy and bright golden brown. For school she wore it in bunches, because of the school rule about pupils not

41

having hair all over their face, but for the audition she had let it loose. 'I am *really* suited to Hermia. Hermia is my part. My uncle said so. He said, "Of couse, Hermia is your part." However, there is no point in sighing for the moon. One has to be realistic and take what is on offer. That's what my uncle says. You can't afford to be too choosy; not until you're an established star.'

'And just when do you suppose, in your case, that that is likely to be?' inquired Barge, cosily.

'Oh, not for years yet! I've a long way to go.'

'Well, do let us know when you get there, won't you? I'm sure we shall all be most interested. Shan't we?' said Barge. They nodded, solemnly.

'Of course, I do realize,' said Melanie, 'that I have an advantage, having an uncle who is in the profession.'

Barge snorted, rudely. She looked around at the others. 'Does anyone get the feeling,' she said, 'that we are wasting our time? I mean, one can hardly be expected to compete,' said Barge, 'with someone who has an *uncle* in the *profession*'.

'I haven't even read the play,' said Jo.

Nobody, it seemed, had read the play – except, of course, Melanie. Melanie had sat up until midnight, or so she claimed, studying it with her uncle.

'Can anyone tell me why we are bothering to stay?' demanded Barge.

It did seem a bit pointless, but as Fij said, 'Strange things *have* been known to happen.' And as Mrs Elliott had said, one should always be prepared to have a go.

In fact, as it turned out, the sixth former who was directing them, Wendy Armstrong, didn't seem particularly to care whether anyone had read the play or not.

42

She seemed to take it for granted that everybody would know what it was about.

To Jo's horror, however, she announced that 'What we are going to do, we are going to start off with a bit of singing . . . *Ye spotted snakes.* Just one verse, that's all. My colleague here has very kindly written some music for us, which she is going to play through a couple of times on the piano so that you can learn the tune. Then I'm going to have you out here, individually, and see what you can do.'

Jo very nearly turned and ran. If she had known it was going to be singing she woud never have come. Melanie, too, obviously felt somewhat aggrieved.

'This isn't the way that it's done!' she hissed. 'If they'd wanted singers they should have said so.'

Jo sat listening, glumly, as Laurel Bustamente trundled herself out to the front and began warbling.

Ye spotted snakes with double tongue, warbled Laurel,
Thorny hedgehogs be not seen;
Newts and blind worms, do no wrong;
Come not near our Fairy Queen.

Laurel's voice was not untuneful – 'But she's too *fat*,' hissed Melanie. 'Whoever saw a fat fairy?'

Fij was next. Fij had a voice like fingernails scraping on a blackboard – 'And anyway, she's too *tall* . . . be all right if they had a Fairy Beanstalk.'

Barge just bellowed, loud and confident and totally unmelodious: Bozzy's voice cracked in the middle: Melanie, the pro, smiled gamely as she wandered ear-splittingly through a variety of keys: Jo started off on the wrong note and determinedly stayed on it, producing what she considered to be quite an interesting difference

43

of opinion between herself and the piano. A bit like modern music, she thought.

The second years then trooped out, one after another, and showed how it ought to be done: all six of them were in the junior choir. The looks of triumph mingled with pity which they bestowed upon the first years were really quite insufferable.

After that they had to read a short scene, with Wendy Armstrong reading the part of Titania, but by now the stuffing had been quite knocked out of them. Only Melanie was able to pull herself together sufficiently to give a performance. The way she sprang smartly forward and delivered her line – 'And I!' – did the form credit. They all agreed, afterwards, that if any of them stood a chance it would be Melanie. Even Barge seemed inclined to forgive her for all her boasting about her uncle: she had at least given the second years something to think about. Melanie, however, shook her head and said 'You feel it in your bones when you're going to get a part.'

So much for Melanie's bones. Next morning, on the notice board, the cast list was pinned up: Melanie was playing Cobweb, Jo was playing Peaseblossom, Fij was Mustard Seed and Bozzy was Moth. Barge and Laurel were 'Attendant Fairies'. A black girl from the second year was playing Puck, while all the rest were attendants along with Barge and Laurel.

On the whole, the second years were not best pleased. As one of them somewhat querulously demanded, 'What do they want that load of screech owls for? They're all tone deaf!'

'A bad workman,' declared Melanie, loftily, 'always blames his tools; whereas a good *actor*,' she said, 'can rise above them. At least,' she added, in confidence to Jo, 'that's what my uncle says.'

Jo could only hope for the audience's sake that Melanie's uncle was right.

5

'Did you see?' cried Fij, as Jo, one morning, came into the classroom.

'See what?' Jo dumped her bag with an ungracious *thunk* on to her desk lid. She was not feeling in the mood for bright conversation – or for guessing games. When she and Matty had got on the bus that morning Julie-Ann had been there. They had all had to stand as far as the station, when as usual lots of people had got off, and Julie-Ann had instantly bagged the only double seat. It was just the sort of mean, sneaky sort of thing she was prone to do. Anybody with even the tiniest little grain of sensitivity would have taken one of the single ones and left the double for Jo and Matty. As it was, Matty had sat next to Julie-Ann leaving Jo all by herself, three rows back. It was just so incon*siderate*.

'The notice board,' urged Fij.

'What about it?'

'There's a notice on it!'

'There's always notices on it.'

'Yes, but this is an *interesting* notice.'

Jo wrestled for a moment with her grumpiness. Grudgingly she said: 'So what's it about?'

'Netball.'

'Oh?'

'You're in the Under-13s!'

'*I* am?' Jo's face grew slowly crimson beneath its freckles. '*Me*? Are you sure? What position?'

'Goal defence.'

Goal defence; it wasn't her favourite position, but any position was worth it, just to be in the team. Anxiously she said: 'What about you?'

'I'm in, so's Nadge. Bozzy and Barge are reserves.'

Jo hoped that Bozzy and Barge wouldn't mind being only reserves when she, a mere new girl, was actually playing in the team. She hoped they wouldn't hold it against her. They both tended to be rather jealous of what they perceived as their rights: girls who had Come Up from the Homestead were definitely a cut above those who had come from other places.

She went down later in the day to check (and to gloat, just a little) and sure enough, there it was – *Goal Defence: Joanne Jameson* – printed in Elizabeth Grey's neat, bold capitals for everyone to see. Wait till she told Matty!

It was only then that it came to her: Matty hadn't even been put down as reserve. . . . She was so ashamed at not having noticed immediately that she couldn't think what to say. Fortunately Matty seemed quite genuinely not to care. She had just gone to her first meeting of the photography club and was full of talk about the camera she was going to get when it was her birthday. She also wanted to know whether Jo's dad, who quite often had letters from abroad, would save his foreign stamps for her.

'It doesn't matter if some of them are the same, I can always swop them.'

Swop them with Julie-Ann, thought Jo; but because she was feeling guilty she promised that she would ask.

She did so that evening, when all the family were sitting round the kitchen table eating supper.

'For Matty,' promised her dad, 'I will make a great effort to remember.'

Jo's dad was the vaguest and most disorganized of people. He might know all about antiques but he knew next to nothing about keeping accounts or answering letters or having a proper filing system. It was left to her mum to see to all that. It was lucky that Jo's mum had trained as an accountant and had what people called 'a good head for business' or the family would have gone bankrupt years ago.

'Shall I write you a big notice?' said Jo. 'SAVE STAMPS FOR MATTY?'

'How is Matty?' said Mrs Jameson. 'Is she getting on all right?'

'Yes, she's in the choir.' Jo hadn't told the family about trying for the choir, any more than she had told them about having to sing in *A Midsummer Night's Dream*. Jo's voice was a family joke. Her grandmother, once, when Jo had been singing along with the radio, had clapped her hands over her ears and cried, 'Somebody fetch an oil can, the child's throat has gone rusty!'

'Matty's in the choir,' said Jo, 'and I'm in the netball team.'

'Ooh! Screech! The *net*ball team!' Tom snatched up a bread roll and with a little high-pitched squeak lobbed it across the table at Andy. Andy said, 'Shut up!' and lobbed it back. Andy, being almost sixteen, wasn't as stupid as Tom, who was still at the stage of thinking it amusing to mock anything he considered 'girls' stuff'. It made Jo want to hit him; but then if she did he only mocked even more, covering his head with his hands and

48

giving loud pretend screeches of terror, which made her even madder so that in the end she lost all control and started clubbing and thumping, and even, on one terrible occasion, clawing and kicking and tearing at his hair, so that she had had to be pulled off. Needless to say, Tom had been quite insufferable after that.

'Fighting like a *girl*!' he'd jeered.

Boys, Jo sometimes thought, were nothing but a pain. They were all right when they got to Andy's age but up until then they ought to be kept locked away, preferably in cages in the middle of a desert, so that decent civilized people didn't have to be bothered by them.

Every Thursday after school, Jo had to stay behind for extra gym classes. On Wednesdays after school there were rehearsals for *A Midsummer Night's Dream*, and on Tuesdays *before* school, which meant setting her alarm clock a whole hour earlier than usual, there was team practice with Elizabeth Grey. It was a very serious business, at Peter's – or at any rate, in Miss Nelligan's house – being in a netball team. As well as the early morning sessions, when it was just the Under-13s, there were lunch-time matches against the Under-14s on alternate Mondays.

The early-morning sessions caused much grumbling amongst a few of the less dedicated. These were the second years, who had been in the team last year and resented having to go through the same routines all over again.

Two of them, Jan Hammond and Katy Wells, didn't turn up one morning. Jan said afterwards that she had overslept: Katy said she had missed her train. Next Monday, when they had their practice match, Elizabeth Grey left them out and put Barge and Bozzy in their

49

place. She said, 'I'm very well aware that netball is only a game, and that games are about enjoying oneself, but the fact is that if you're *not* enjoying yourselves then you oughtn't to be on the team. I don't want people who find it a drag, because we find *them* a drag. You either commit yourselves wholeheartedly or not at all.'

Jan and Katy sulked and mumbled but they didn't miss another practice. They still muttered, though, when Elizabeth was out of earshot.

'We *did* all this last year,' they muttered, and 'Some people are just so *slow*' – meaning, presumably, Jo and Fij. Not even the second years could accuse Nadge of being slow, though they would probably like to have done so.

People in the same house weren't supposed to compete, but the rivalry between the first and second years was deep and bitter and of long standing. Back in the Homestead, it seemed, the second years – who had then been Homestead Class 5 – had once cheated at a sports day, with the result, according to Barge, that they had gone waltzing off with all the chief prizes when at least half of them ought by rights to have gone to Class 4, now the first years. Naturally the second years hotly disputed this version of events, but as Bozzy said, they would, wouldn't they? People who were capable of cheating were hardly very likely to make much distinction between fact and fiction.

'Of course, you know what their trouble is,' said Fij, as she and Jo wandered back across from the Field after a lunch-time game. 'They're just mad because of not getting into the Under-14s. That's where they think they *ought* to be.'

'I don't think they ought to be anywhere,' said Jo,

50

'carrying on the way they do. I think Barge and Bozzy ought to be in the team in place of them.'

Barge and Bozzy had been exceedingly gracious about Jo playing goal defence and them being only reserves.

'It must be so wretched for you,' had oozed Barge, 'being new to all our little ways and having to play with *cheats*.'

'Although, of course,' had added Bozzy, 'it is for the good of the House.'

'And besides, as you are a new girl you have only our word for it that they are cheats so possibly it may not bother you as it would us.'

Jo had earnestly assured them that it *did* bother her, but she was doing her best to rise above it – 'I keep telling myself that it's my duty . . . for the sake of the House.'

'Oh, well, abso*lutely*,' had gushed Barge. 'I do so *agree*.'

It was possible, Jo had discovered, to get on quite amicably with Barge so long as one did nothing to upset her own view of her importance. Jo had no objection to her being important, if that was what she wanted. Unfortunately, some of the second years did: that was where much of the trouble arose.

'Listen—' Fij linked her arm companionably through Jo's. 'I've been told to ask you something . . . Barge says, do you want to join us?'

Jo stopped. 'Join the Gang?'

'Well, you would have to be probationary just at first. I think you will agree,' said Fij, 'that that is only reasonable.'

'Oh! Quite,' said Jo.

'But we think that you would fit. It would mean that we could be four again. We were always four, until Mo left. We've been looking for someone else. So we had this meeting at break and we decided,' said Fij, 'to ask you.' Disarmingly, she added: 'We couldn't think of anyone else. Naomi is far too clever, and anyway Gerry and Prue have already grabbed her, and Melanie keeps going on about her uncle until one could scream and throttle her, and Ash is such a *bore*, whereas, as Barge says, you are not *desperately* clever, and you don't seem to have any tiresome relatives, and we don't on the whole find you boring, so that one way or another, and taken all in all, as Stanny keeps saying in her loathsome maths classes, you do *appear*,' said Fij, 'to be more Our Sort of Person than anyone else.'

'Thank you very much,' stammered Jo.

'Not at all.' Fij inclined her head, graciously. 'Credit where credit is due, that is what I always say. Besides, if we don't have you it will have to be Lol, which will lower the whole *tone* of the Gang, but really, apart from her there is only Claire Kramer, who is decidedly odd, I think you will agree. I mean, doing ballet is one thing, but keeping oneself so *very* much to oneself is hardly what could be called socially acceptable behaviour. It makes one feel as if one has some particularly gruesome sort of disease. Not that I am saying that you are *perfect*.'

Jo hastily, and with due humility, agreed that she wasn't.

'But even though you are new and undeniably have some peculiarly annoying habits, such as for instance *bouncing* every time you sit down so that my desk shakes and makes me feel sick – I hope you don't mind my mentioning it? I think it is one's social duty,' said Fij, 'to draw people's attention to these little foibles. Anyway, apart from that you do otherwise appear to be relatively normal, which is more than can be said for Lol. I don't really consider it normal,' said Fij, 'to resemble a cream *bun*. So. There you have it. In a nutshell. To be or not to be, and so on and so forth . . . whether you wish to avail yourself of our offer or whether, perchance, you have some other prospect in view?'

Jo shook herself. She had been mesmerized, just for a moment, by the high-flown tone of Fij's language. In none of Miss Lloyd's English classes had she betrayed any signs of commanding such an erudite vocabulary. In fact only the other day she had creased everyone by pronouncing the word fatigue as 'fatty gew'.

'I mean,' said Fij, reverting to normal, 'it's entirely up to you.'

If it *were* up to her, thought Jo, she would have no hesitation. But there was Matty to think of. How could she join without Matty?'

'Naturally, if you feel that you are too superior—'

Quickly, Jo found her tongue. 'It's not that! But there's Matty, you see.'

'Matty McShane?' Fij sounded surprised. 'Is she still your friend? Barge said—'

'What did Barge say?'

'Oh! Well—' Fij looked uncomfortable. 'Nothing, really. She just said she thought she was going with Jool.'

'Well, she's not! Jool just tags on. Matty and I have been friends for *years*.'

'I see. That does rather alter things. I wouldn't have asked you,' said Fij, 'if I'd known. Trust Barge to go and get it wrong.'

'I suppose' – Jo said it rather timidly – 'I suppose we couldn't both join?'

'Well, not really – it would make us more of a *crowd*,'

said Fij, 'than a gang. And in any case, it would be an odd number. Besides, four is exclusive: five is just a rabble. Like that dreadful mob in the second year. We shouldn't want to become like *them*.'

'No,' Jo said, meekly. 'I can see that.'

Fij sighed. 'I suppose it will have to be Lol . . . she's been trying to squidge her way in ever since she heard that Mo was leaving.'

Because of dawdling, and taking their time changing, Jo and Fij arrived slightly late for the double period of Home Ec. which took up the rest of the day. Mrs Dyer was easygoing (unlike Miss Lloyd, who was capable of turning nasty) and simply told them to 'Hurry up and find yourselves a partner and sit down', but when Jo turned to look for Matty she found to her immense indignation that the interloper, the horrid tubby little interloper known as Julie-Ann Gillon, had gone and usurped her place. Matty at least had the grace to look the other way. The interloper just stared, brazenly, and said, 'I'm working with Matty to-day.' Jo wanted to pick up a mixing bowl and smash it over her stupid head. She looked round for Fij, but Fij, already, had been greedily snapped up by Big Lol. The only person left was Naomi.

Naomi was all right, just rather serious and solemn – not the sort to throw rock cakes at people, or smash mixing bowls over their heads – but the point was that Jo shouldn't have *been* with her; she should have been with Matty. She was beginning to loathe Julie-Ann. Self-important, pobble-eyed creature. Her teeth stuck out, and so did her ears, and she scuffed her feet as she walked . . . scuff, scuff, scuff, like the old tramp woman known as the Newspaper Lady from her habit of shuffling the streets wrapped in old newspaper.

Probably where Julie-Ann would end up if she weren't careful. And why did she wear her hair in that absurd topknot? It looked ridiculous. Matty had beautiful hair, all thick and ringleted. Matty was *pretty*. Julie-Ann looked like a horrible blubber-mouthed goldfish. She decided that on the way home tonight she would pointedly ignore Julie-Ann.

As it happened, it wasn't so much a question of Jo ignoring Julie-Ann as of Julie-Ann and Matty ignoring Jo: they prattled together the whole bus journey about some stupid camera club competition they were going to enter when Matty had her camera. They were going to take photographs of *pavements*.

'What is the point of photographing pavements?' said Jo.

'To get the texture,' said Matty.

'Pavements,' explained Julie-Ann – kindly, as if Jo were a cretin – 'are all different.'

'*Paving* stones—'

'*Con*crete—'

'*Tess*ellated—'

Tessellated! Jo shook her fringe disdainfully into her eyes. They'd never even heard the word until they'd done it in CDT the other day.

She had to wait till they got off the bus (leaving Julie-Ann to continue for another two stops) before she had Matty to herself.

'Nice flowers,' said Matty, as they turned into Winterbourne Avenue. She hung over the hedge of the big house on the corner, sniffing enthusiastically. 'Pretty. Didn't know you got them at this time of year. Wonder what they are? Some sort of rose, they look like. Dog rose? Wild rose?'

Since when had Matty been interested in roses? It was just a ploy to keep Jo from asking the question which Matty must know very well she was going to ask.

'Christmas rose? I bet that's what it is. I bet it's a Christmas rose.'

'Why?' said Jo. 'It's not Christmas.' And then, before Matty could start off all over again (*briar* rose, *miniature* rose) 'What did you go and partner *her* for?'

'Had to partner someone.' Matty, affecting unconcern, swung her bag. 'Thought you weren't coming.'

'You knew I was coming!'

'No, I didn't,' said Matty. 'You go off places with other people—'

'Only Fij. We had a netball practice.'

'You're always having netball practices.'

'Well, you're always having choir!'

'Only once a week. Anyway,' said Matty, 'even when I do partner you you only mess around. Look what happened last time, with those rock cakes.'

'Heavens!' said Jo. 'You're not still on about *that*?'

'You ruined them,' said Matty.

It was true: she had ruined them. It couldn't be denied. But really, she thought, what was a rock cake? It could hardly be considered of monumental importance in the universal scheme of things.

'What it is,' said Matty, 'you're just not interested. And when you're not interested you don't bother to try.'

They stopped, as they reached the gate to Matty's house.

'Are *you* interested?' said Jo.

'Yes.' Matty clicked open the gate and closed it behind her, defiantly. 'I *like* cooking.'

Jo waited a moment, then called after her: 'Hey! Mat!'

Matty turned, slowly. 'What?'

'Fancy going to the new baths? Over Hollyfield?' The new baths at Hollyfield were one of the wonders of the modern world: they had a *wave machine*. They also had a poolside cafeteria where you could sit and drink Coke and watch other people when you'd come out. 'Be fun,' said Jo. 'We could go on Saturday, get the green bus. Only takes half an hour.'

'Really I'm saving up to buy a flash for my camera,' said Matty. Her camera that she hadn't even *got* yet. 'But I s'pose we could. If you want.'

'We ought,' said Jo. 'We haven't done anything together for ages. Not properly.'

'All right. Saturday morning, 'leven o'clock. You just make sure you're ready.'

'I'll be ready,' said Jo.

6

A letter had come for Jo from her French penfriend, returning *her* letter all covered in red ink corrections as if it were a school exercise.

I think you will like me to make this corrections, he wrote. *I will like you to make also corrections.*

At the end of the letter was a long PS:

In French we do not say, ami de plume. We say, correspondant. But when you write it for you it is correspondante, and when you write ami, it is amie. I hope you will understand this corrections. It is for male and female. This is of importance in the French tongue. I think it is not of so importance in English. Please tell me in your letter, I wish to learn from you.

Horrid pedantic thing! Jo leaned across the table and dropped the letter on Tom's toast.

'I think you ought to have this,' she said. 'He can be your ami now . . . you're the one that speaks all the French.'

At the end of English on Wednesday afternoon Miss Lloyd said she wanted them all to pair off and choose a project which interested them and which they would like to work on together in their spare time and in study periods.

'We discussed this last week, so I shall expect you all by now to have had some ideas.'

Jo not only had no ideas, she had completely forgotten

that Miss Lloyd had ever mentioned projects in the first place. This was because immediately after English on a Wednesday she had to rush off to a *Dream* rehearsal. She hissed at Matty as they left the classroom together, 'Think of something! Tell me tomorrow!' Matty, she thought, gave her a somewhat startled look, but she didn't have time to say any more: Matty was carried off in the general surge along the corridor, Jo turned left up the stairs, making for the small hall where rehearsals were held.

Next morning, they met as usual to walk to the bus together.

'Did you think of something?' said Jo.

'I thought of something ages ago.'

'Good! What?'

Matty fiddled with the strap on her school bag. It had double cords running through a large red bead which you could slide up and down according to whether you wanted the cords to be longer or shorter. Shuffle shuffle shuffle went the bead, back and forth.

'You're not going to like this,' said Matty.

'It's all right,' said Jo. 'We can do whatever you want.'

'Thing is–' shuffle shuffle went the bead – 'I've said I'll do it with Jool.'

'*Jool*?' Jo felt almost, for a moment, as if someone had punched her. Her stomach went all cold and clammy. With trembly hand, she pushed her fringe out of her eyes.

'See, what we're doing,' said Matty, gabbling rather on account of being embarrassed, 'we're doing this thing on slavery, and I thought you wouldn't want to do a thing on slavery, so—'

'Why wouldn't I?' said Jo. Her voice came out very

small and tight. 'Why wouldn't I want to do a thing on slavery?'

'Well, I mean, it's not – like – well! You know,' said Matty. 'I didn't think you'd be interested.'

'You could've *asked* me,' said Jo.

'I would've, if you'd been there, but you're never around. And in any case,' said Matty, 'it was Jool's idea, and I'm really sorry, but you *aren't* ever around, you keep going off doing things, and she did come and ask me, and—'

'And *what*?'

'I never know with you, these days . . . you're not the same as you used to be.'

'No,' said Jo. 'and neither are you!'

Carelessly, as she arranged things on her desk after morning assembly, she said to Fij: 'Got anyone to do your project with?'

'Lol,' said Fij. She pulled the slightest of faces as she said it. Laurel Bustamente had achieved her ambition: she was now an official member of the Laing Gang. Jo could have been a member if it hadn't been for misplaced loyalty to Matty, who didn't *deserve* loyalty, not the way she'd been behaving of late. 'How about you?' said Fij. 'Who're you doing it with?'

'Haven't decided yet.' Jo concentrated on ranging her pens, pencils, ruler and rubber neatly along the top of her desk. 'What with all the multitudinous things that go on in one's life' – she gave a little laugh: a silly little snickering bray – 'I just don't seem to have had the time to think about it.'

Just as Jo had taken it for granted that she would be doing her project with Matty, Miss Lloyd took it for granted that everyone, by now, would have chosen a partner and decided on a subject. Two cross red blotches appeared on her cheeks when she discovered that Jo had done neither. Red blotches appeared on Jo's cheeks, too, but Jo's blotches were blotches of shame. Back in Juniors, she had never been without a partner. Even if Matty had been away and Trish and Laura had gone together, there had always been someone eager to claim her. Sometimes there had even been a fight over her – *I'm* having Jammy!' 'No, you're not, she promised *me*!'

'So who's the other odd one out?' Miss Lloyd's eyes, popping dangerously in their sockets, angrily scanned the class. 'Who else doesn't have a partner?'

Claire Kramer put her hand up.

'Very well!' snapped Miss Lloyd. 'Get yourselves together and get something worked out. I want to know by this time tomorrow what you're doing.'

Claire was someone who kept herself very much to herself. She was always polite, but she didn't seem to feel the need to belong to a group or have any special friends of her own. Occasionally she went round with Melanie and Ash, but quite often she just sat and read a book or darned ballet shoes (Jo had never heard of anyone darning *ballet* shoes before) or simply disappeared somewhere by herself. Jo was aware that there were some people who didn't like her. Bozzy and Barge thought she was aloof and anti-social, Matty and Julie-Ann said she gave herself airs. They only said that because Claire didn't rush around shrieking and carrying on like everyone else. Since she couldn't partner Matty, and Fij had been bagged by Big Lol, Jo thought that she would sooner work with Claire than any of the others. At least Claire was her own person.

At break she hurried to catch up with her before she could do one of her vanishing acts.

'Are you going up the refectory?'

'I'm going over to the Field.'

'All right,' said Jo. She didn't mind missing out on her mid-morning bun. The other day she had come across a great horrid lump of candied peel, as well as all the loathsome currants. 'I'll come with you, then we can talk about this project. What do you think we ought to do? Have you got any ideas?'

'I'm going to do a project on ballet,' said Claire.

'Oh.' Jo was slightly taken aback: she had expected *some* consultation. But Claire, although quiet, was always very certain about everything. 'Self-possessed' was what Mrs Stanley had called her the other day, in maths. She had said, 'You're very self-possessed, aren't you, Claire?' in amused tones, as if self-possession were a quality she approved of.

'Ok, then,' said Jo. 'We'll do a project on ballet. The only trouble is' – she scraped her hair behind her ears, wishing it were a bit longer so that she could tie it in a pony tail like Claire's – 'I don't know very much about it. Of course, I have *seen* some.' She wouldn't want Claire to think she was a total ignoramus. 'I've seen that one where there's a man dressed up as a woman and he does this dance in clogs.'

'*La Fille mal Gardée*,' said Claire.

'Yes. I liked that one.'

Claire smiled. Jo thought that perhaps everyone who didn't know very much about ballet said that they had seen that one and had liked it. Perhaps it was the sort of ballet that people who didn't know about ballet *would* like, while people who knew about it didn't think much of it.

'Do you like it?' she said.

'Not as much as some,' said Claire.

'What ones do you like?'

'*Petrushka* is my favourite at the moment, but I expect that's because I'm studying it.'

Jo had never heard of *Petrushka*. She rummaged through her mind for any other ballets she could think of.

'What about *Swan Lake*?' she said. 'Do you like that?'

'Yes,' said Claire. 'I like *Swan Lake*.'

'That's the one with the – ah – mm, swans,' said Jo.

Claire giggled. Jo grew pink – and then she giggled, too.

'Now I s'pose you'll tell me it's wart hogs, or something?'

'The Dance of the Little Wart Hogs. . . .' Claire seemed on the point of demonstrating, then at the last minute changed her mind. Unlike Melanie, who was for ever doing her acting all over the classroom and the cloakroom and just wherever she happened to be – the gym, the netball court, the main corridor, it was all one to Melanie – Claire never showed off in public. Jo said, 'Go on!' but she only laughed and shook her head, so that her blond pony tail swished to and fro.

'Not here.'

'Why not? Nobody's watching.'

'Yes, they are – you are!'

'Well, but if we're doing this project,' said Jo, 'I need to know, don't I? How can I do a project about ballet if I'm going round thinking Swan Lake's got swans in it 'stead of wart hogs?'

Claire walked in silence for a few minutes.

'I suppose . . .' She looked at Jo, gravely, out of large

greeny-grey eyes. 'I suppose you could always come round. If you wanted to.'

'To your place?'

'So that we can work on it. I've got lots of books,' said Claire. 'We could look things up – dates and things.'

'When?' Jo tried not to sound too eager. Nobody had ever been round to Claire's place – nobody even knew where she lived. Barge had said, caustically, that it was bound to be somewhere 'fearsomely grand . . . up on the hill with the nobs.'

'Saturday morning?' said Claire.

'All right.' Jo nodded. Claire wasn't anywhere near as stand-offish as some people made out; not once you actually got talking to her.

'I'll give you the address later,' said Claire.

Jo was surprised, on Saturday morning, when she got off the bus in the centre of town and made her way through a maze of twisty side streets to the address which Claire had handed to her on a scrap of paper, last thing Friday evening. Barge couldn't have been more wrong: Turnpike Lane was nowhere near Petersham Hill with its big detached houses where (so it was rumoured) millionaires and pop stars hid themselves away for secrecy. Instead, it was down near the market where the stallholders had their barrows and the streets were full of rotting cabbage stalks and squashed tomatoes. Jo had been to the market, lots of times, but she had never penetrated beyond it, to the maze of Victorian terraces which lay behind.

Claire's house was an 'end of terrace', very neat and trim, with polished brasswork and clipped privet hedge, and tiny as a dolls' house. Her bedroom was about the size of Jo's at home – in other words, 'like a broom cupboard', as Jo was wont to grumble, somewhat bitterly. The difference was that at home in Winterbourne Avenue Jo's bedroom was the smallest (being number three she was stuck with it until such time as Andy went off to college and she and Tom could both move up one). In Turnpike Lane, Claire proudly explained, 'This was my mum and dad's room . . . they gave it to me when I started ballet, so I could have somewhere to practise.'

Jo's face must have betrayed her – *practise*? in *that* tiny space? – for Claire blushed and quickly added, 'Only barre work, of course.' Jo nodded, sagely, to show that she understood, though she wasn't at all sure that she did.

By the time she left Claire at twelve o'clock (Claire had a ballet class starting at one) Jo knew a great deal more about ballet than she had before. She knew all about its origins in France, in the eighteenth century, she knew about Diaghileff and the Russians, about Nijinsky and Pavlova and Leonid Massine, she knew about Petrushka, she even knew what barre work was.

'These are pliés . . . these are battements. . . .'

Jo felt pretty sure that *she* could do pliés and battements. She couldn't wait to get home so that she could try them out, upstairs in her broom cupboard. In fact, an idea was forming in her mind . . . if Matty could have a camera for *her* birthday. . . .

'Jo!' Mrs Jameson was waiting for her, at the front door. She sounded accusing, as if Jo had done something wrong. 'Had you forgotten you were supposed to be going swimming with Matty?'

Matty! *Oh.* Jo clapped a horrified hand to her mouth.

'I think you'd better go and apologise to her . . . *straight away*.'

It was too late: Matty wasn't there. Miles came to the door and said she'd gone into town with her mother to do some shopping. Jo drooped.

'I'll tell her you called,' said Miles.

'Tell her I'm really sorry,' said Jo.

'Really sorry.'

'For letting her down.'

'Letting her down.'

He didn't have to keep *repeating* everything, thought Jo. It just made it sound all the worse.

She did her best to comfort herself, as half-heartedly she did pliés in the broom cupboard, with the reflection that really and truly it was all Matty's own fault: if she hadn't chosen to do her project with Julie-Ann, Jo wouldn't have had any *need* to go round to Claire's. The more one thought about it, it was actually very *mean* of Matty.

It still didn't stop her feeling bad.

7

'Do you think,' said Jo, as she munched her way through the last of her breakfast cornflakes, 'that I could do ballet?'

'Do I think what?' said her mother. She was busy dumping dirty dishes in the sink, clattering and clunking and swishing the hot water.

'Do you think that I could do ballet?'

'Ballet?' Mrs Jameson repeated the word, vaguely. Her mind, quite obviously, was elsewhere.

'*Ballet*,' said Jo.

'Ballet.' A pile of plates cascaded into the sink. Water sprayed the kitchen floor. Mrs Jameson was better at doing accounts than she was at doing housework. 'You mean. . . .'

'*Dancing*,' said Jo. As in plié: as in battement: as in *Swan Lake*. She wished her mother would hurry up and pay attention before the others came crashing back. She had purposely waited till they were out of the room, Andy outside pumping up his bicycle tyres and Tom in his bedroom searching for a lost football boot. There were some things you just couldn't talk about in front of brothers. Even Andy wasn't above pulling her leg on occasion. He wasn't as sexist as Tom, but it sometimes seemed to Jo that whatever she got enthusiastic about – like last year, for instance, when for a short while she had thought she might take up knitting and had actually managed to do 13.5 cm. of a stripy scarf before she had grown bored and given it to her mother to use as a table mat – Andy thought it the funniest thing on earth. *Jo – knitting. Jo – dancing.*

'Could I,' she said, 'do you think?'

'Well, I suppose . . .' Her mother cast round, distractedly, for a tea towel. 'If you really wanted.'

'There's a girl at school, Claire Kramer, who goes to Miss Lintott's.'

'And what is Miss Lintott's?'

'Just about the best ballet school in the whole of Petersham. Maybe' – so Claire had said – 'in the whole *country*.'

'That's a mighty big claim!'

'Claire says she wouldn't go anywhere else if you paid her.'

'Is anyone likely to pay her?'

'They will, one day,' said Jo. 'She's incredibly gifted.' She knew that Claire was incredibly gifted because she had overheard Lucy Abott, one of the fifth formers who was doing the Greek dancing at the start of *A Midsummer Night's Dream*, telling somebody. *That child*, she had said, *that Claire Kramer, she's incredibly gifted.*

'So could I?' said Jo.

'Go to Miss Lintott's?'

'With Claire.'

'I'll tell you what.' Deftly, Mrs Jameson removed a tea towel from a pile of ironing sitting on the kitchen table. 'I'll make you a promise . . . if you still want to do it by the end of term, we'll pay for a course of lessons as your Christmas present. How about that?'

Jo pulled a face. Christmas was an awfully long time to

wait – it was more than two months away. Jo knew what her mother was thinking. She was thinking, this is just one of her fads. Like the white mice, which had had to be given away, and the knitting, which had ended up as a table mat. By Christmas she would want to do something quite different. Water skiing, or learning to fly.

'If you're really serious,' said Mrs Jameson, 'you'd better start saving up your money to buy ballet shoes and things.'

'All right,' said Jo, 'I will!'

If Matty could save up to buy bits and pieces for her camera, Jo could save up to buy ballet shoes.

Relations between Jo and Matty were a bit strained just at the moment. On Sunday morning Jo had been in the garden, playing two-ball against the garage door (dividing herself into teams, one team being her and Fij, the other Barge and Bozzy) when Matty had appeared. Matty had also started playing two-ball, against her own garage door. They hadn't exactly ignored each other – when one of Jo's balls had gone flying into the McShanes' flower bed, Matty had politely thrown it back to her: when one of Matty's had shot out into the road, it was Jo who had gone running off to fetch it for her: in each case, very gravely and with immense formality, they had said their thank yous – but there was never any suggestion that they should join forces and play together, as normally they would have done.

It wasn't until Mr McShane opened his garage door and told Matty to stop throwing balls at it – 'Garage doors aren't meant to have balls thrown at them' – that Jo said, 'You can come and play against my door, if you like.' Matty's dad had looked at her as if suspecting her of impudence. Matty had said, 'I didn't want to play any more anyway. I'm going in.' She hadn't invited Jo to go in with her.

Now it was Monday morning and Jo without the least idea whether Matty was going to be there as usual, waiting for her – Matty was almost always ready before Jo – or whether, for the first time in practically living memory, they would be going their separate ways to school.

She was relieved, when she went rushing down the garden path, to find Matty standing there. She hated quarrelling. Some people did it all the time – Trish and Laura, for instance, they had always been falling out, and Barge and Bozzy, only the other day, had threatened to punch each other's stupid faces in (they had made it up again afterwards). Jo and Matty had never quarrelled; not like that. The very idea was quite horrid.

'I'm really sorry about Saturday,' said Jo.

''s all right,' said Matty. 'Doesn't matter.'

'P'raps' – Jo suggested it, tentatively – 'p'raps we could go *this* Saturday?'

'I can't this Saturday. We're going to my Gran's.'

'Oh.'

There was a silence.

'Go Sunday,' said Matty.

'I can't Sunday. . . .' On Sunday the Jamesons were visiting Jo's gran. 'But we ought to go *some* time.'

'Yeah,' said Matty, 'we ought.'

They didn't quarrel and threaten to push each other's faces in.

For all that, things were not the same as they had been and it was no use pretending that they were. They still sat next to each other in art and music, but it was accepted,

70

now, that in Home Ec. Matty would work with Julie-Ann rather than Jo. They were doing their projects with other people, they were members of different clubs, they even went round with different groups in the playground.

Matty and Julie-Ann had attached themselves to Nadge and her mob, which consisted of Nadge's special friend Lee Powell (the one who had given the black power salute on the first day of term) and three or four others who had all been in the Homestead. Matty didn't seem to mind being the only new girl amongst them: she was accepted because of Julie-Ann. There wasn't any reason why Jo shouldn't have joined them if she'd wanted, except that they hadn't invited her and she was too proud to ask. Nadge was always friendly but Lee Powell could be funny, specially with white girls. She was very aggressive, was Lee; always getting into fights and quick to take offence. Matty said she was 'OK when you got to know her' but Jo wasn't at all sure that she wanted to.

Mostly, these days, Jo knocked about with Melanie Peach and Ashley Wilkerson, plus Claire when Claire felt inclined. Jo had discovered what she did on those occasions when she disappeared: she went up to the music rooms to find a spare piano to practise on. Jo wondered, if she was as keen on music as all that, why she didn't have private lessons, but then she thought about it and she thought that maybe Claire's parents couldn't afford it. They only lived in such a *very* tiny little house, and they were already paying for Claire to have all those dancing classes. The dancing classes were expensive; Jo knew this because she had secretly written away for a prospectus from Miss Lintott. She had thought that perhaps while she was waiting for Christmas to come she might be able to afford to pay for some classes herself, but even just one a week was more than her pocket money. Miss Lintott must be *very* exclusive.

'She is,' said Melanie, who knew about these things. 'My mum tried to get me in there once but she wouldn't take me. She said she might be able to teach me how to do the steps but she could never make a dancer of me.'

It was funny about Melanie. In spite of being quite insufferable on the subject of My Uncle who is an Actor, and posturing and preening all over the place, spouting her poetry and doing her voice exercises ('Mmmmmmm-MAH-mmmmmmmmmm-MOH-mmmmmmmmm-MEE') she wasn't really what you could call bigheaded. She enjoyed showing off at the things she knew she was good at, but she never claimed to be good at things that other people could do better. If Jo had tried to get in to Miss Lintott's and had been told to go away again she wasn't at all sure that she would be so ready to admit it; but as Melanie said, 'I don't want to be a dancer, so it doesn't really bother me. Claire's obviously ballerina material.'

'You can tell that just by looking at her,' gushed Ashley. Ashley did tend to gush, rather – maybe because she herself was so totally undistinguished. The sort of person who would never get into a games team or come top of an exam or be a leading light in a school society. Jo felt sorry for her, sometimes; but she did wish she wouldn't be quite so in *awe*. Jo thought Claire was absolutely the most fascinating person she had ever met, but she wouldn't lower herself the way Ashley did.

'She's so *tiny*, isn't she? Really dainty. Not just *small*, like the Mouse, but really beautiful.'

72

'It's the way she holds herself,' said Melanie, professional fount of all knowledge when it came to matters theatrical. 'And the way she's proportioned . . . it's very important, for a dancer, the way they're proportioned.'

Jo took to looking at Claire after that to see how her proportions differed from Jo's. She couldn't actually see that they did. In gym one day she stood next to her and tried to measure her legs against Claire's: it didn't seem to Jo that Claire's were any longer or in any way different. Her waist wasn't any smaller – the way she knew that was that they had all had to attend a costume call for the *Dream* and she had seen Claire's measurements written down under "Dancers" – her feet weren't any tinier, or at least only half a size, but then Jo was a few centimetres taller, so that was in proportion, wasn't it?

She bet she could be a dancer just as well as Claire. You could tell that someone like Melanie couldn't, because although Melanie was very pretty and slim she wasn't at all athletic, she hated PE and she couldn't even manage to get over the box in gym. And you could tell that someone like Nadge couldn't, because although Nadge was supple and double-jointed and quite amazingly acrobatic – she could walk on her hands almost the whole length of the playground – she was muscly in the wrong sort of places for ballet, and also she was a bit bow-legged. You obviously couldn't have a bow-legged ballet dancer.

Consciously, Jo began to model herself on Claire. She studied the way that Claire walked – straight-backed, head held high, with her feet ever-so-slightly turned out. She watched the way that Claire sat, the way that Claire gestured, the way that Claire stood and jumped and ran.

She noticed all these things and did her best to copy them, hoping that Claire, in her turn, would notice; hoping that Claire might say, 'Jam, why don't *you* do ballet? You look as if you'd be really good at it,' but Claire never did, she was too self-absorbed. She lived in a world of her own and scarcely seemed aware of what was going on outside.

One day in gym, after they'd been vaulting over the horse, Miss Dyer said, 'Tell me! Has anyone noticed who are the lightest on their feet?'

Julie-Ann said, 'Nadge.' Melanie said, 'Claire.'

'Anyone else?' said Miss Dyer.

'Jammy? I mean, Jo?' said Fij.

'Yes,' said Miss Dyer. 'Jo, Claire and Nadia; those are the ones I would have picked.'

Jo tried to talk about it with Claire, afterwards. 'Some people must be flatfooted . . . clump, clump, clump, like a herd of wallabies thundering about the place.' She'd hoped that Claire might have said something on the lines of, 'Well, of course, *you're* built like a dancer,' but instead she just giggled and said, 'Dance of the Little Wallabies,' and took a few clumping steps along the corridor.

Even when Claire clumped she managed to look graceful. Jo tried clumping that evening, in front of the full-length mirror in the bathroom, but her mother called up the stairs to ask her what on earth she thought she was doing before she had a proper chance to see whether she looked graceful or not.

She had *thought* that she did, but then at the next *Dream* rehearsal all the fairies had to learn a special fairy dance which a girl in the fifth year had made up for them, and Claire was the one who was chosen to demonstrate.

Claire and the other dancers weren't actually going to *do* the fairy dance, they were being a Greek frieze at the beginning, which meant wearing white pleated tunics and striking poses like on Greek vases, but Claire was so used to picking up new routines that it was nothing to her to learn something on the spot and teach it to the reluctant fairy crew.

'*Dance*?' wailed Fij.

'*Me*?' said Barge.

'All of you!' said Wendy, who was directing.

Jo concentrated hard, following Claire's every move. The steps were fairly simple, as befitted non-dancers, but surprisingly difficult to fit into one's head all at once. The first time the fairies tried it out by themselves, without Claire to lead them, Jo suddenly found herself staring straight into Bozzy's face when by rights she should have been looking at the back of her neck. Fortunately the mistake was Bozzy's: she had turned the wrong way. All the people who were watching thought it tremendously funny. Wendy said, 'I rather like that!' and made a note on her director's notepad. How could she like it? thought Jo. They weren't supposed to be a comedy show.

Claire, who was watching, had giggled as much as anybody. It made Jo feel quite cross. It wasn't fair, putting her in with this load of clumsy hippopotamuses – Big Lol, thudding up and down, shaking the floorboards, Barge just *barging*, in her usual bargelike fashion, Bozzy blissfully unaware even now that she had done anything wrong, Fij looking like a demented stick insect, Katy Wells from the second year with her fingers all splayed out like bunches of twigs and her legs going like steamhammers. Jo could only smile at them pityingly and try to remain aloof. (Surely Claire would see that she was in a different class from the others?)

Wendy said, 'Just take them through it once again, would you, Claire? Everybody follow Claire: do it with her.'

By beating Barge at her own game and using her elbows, Jo succeeded in positioning herself immediately behind Claire. She did everything that Claire did, the way that Claire did it. She didn't know what the others did, and she didn't care. *She* knew how to do it without making a fool of herself. There was applause at the end.

'Why is it,' said Michelle Wandres (she of the correspondence club) 'that I always seem to end up watching the same two people? Claire, of course' – Jo edged herself up, closer – 'and Chloë!'

Her? thought Jo.

'*Me*?' said Bozzy. (She still had no idea what she was doing wrong.)

'Claire is so graceful,' said Michelle, 'and Chloë is such a hoot!'

Bozzy's blue eyes popped. With some feeling, afterwards, as they left school together, Jo said, 'You can't place any reliance on the opinion of someone like Michelle Wandres.' She said it as much to comfort herself as Bozzy. Couldn't Michelle *see* that she was a cut above the rest?

'I'm beginning to think I don't particularly want to be in this production anyway,' said Bozzy. 'Not if it means having to sing *and* dance – and why have they cast that great fat wobbling thing as Titania? It's like having Lol as a fairy. Anyone would think they *wanted* people to laugh.'

They were all agreed that the casting was peculiar, to say the very least.

'I mean,' said Bozzy, 'it's all right for you and Melanie, being as you're both quite small and I *suppose* Melanie could be described as prettyish, though you are only what I should call ordinary. In fact I have often thought that your face bears an uncanny resemblance to a squashed apple. I hope you don't mind my saying so?'

'Not at all,' said Jo. 'Please feel quite free.'

'Well, but I wouldn't want you to imagine that I have anything *against* apples because I absolutely don't, especially when they're covered in freckles, and after all there's no reason why a fairy *shouldn't* have freckles, but what – I put it to you! – about the rest of us? Just tell me honestly! Do we *look* like fairies?'

They didn't. Bozzy was too stubby and Barge was too solid and Fij was too thin and too lanky and tall. It was also true that Rachel Jacobs, a fifth former who had been cast as Titania, had a most unfortunate tendency to wobble as she walked. She wasn't just big, she was *enormous*. The sixth former who was playing Oberon was more like Fij, very tall and thin. Far too bony, everyone said. Oberon ought to be lithe and handsome – like Elizabeth Grey. She would have made an excellent Oberon. Instead she was playing Lysander, one of the lovers, which the first years considered a ridiculous piece of miscasting. The lovers were all totally wet, and as far as they were concerned the play would be far better off without them.

'Gross mismanagement,' grumbled Barge. 'Gross,' she added, 'being the operative word in the case of *some* people.'

'I'm afraid it's all one can expect,' said Melanie, patting in lethargic fashion at a yawn, 'when things are left in the hands of amateurs . . . *no* overall vision, *no*

77

artistic feeling . . . just say the words and don't bump into the furniture; it's the only advice I can really give you.'

'Did anyone *ask* for her advice?' said Barge.

'No, and furthermore,' said Fij, 'there isn't going to be any furniture. We're doing it on a bare stage.'

'Which is probably just as well.' Melanie looked kindly at Bozzy. 'It means that all you'll have to do is remember to turn left when you're supposed to turn left and *try* not to fall into the front row of the stalls. It is such a nasty surprise for an audience, having hefty great bodies come crashing down on top of them.'

Bozzy turned scarlet. Barge muttered something about great hefty bodies coming crashing down on Melanie if she didn't stop patronising people. Jo found herself, for once, in sympathy: Melanie just didn't seem to know the meaning of the word tact. Claire was every bit as talented as she was, if not a great deal more so, and she didn't go round lording it over everyone, telling them how they ought to conduct themselves.

8

Because of the project, Jo was seeing more of Claire than she was of Matty. They worked together in the library, and one Saturday morning went to the Central Library in Petersham to see what ballet books they had which weren't already in Claire's collection. They found several and went away with a great pile which Claire said they must read. Mrs Jameson was most impressed when she saw Jo staggering through the door with four fat volumes.

'What's all this? *History of the Dance – Dance Through the Ages – Stories of the Ballets* . . . my goodness! You're really going at it in a big way!'

'It's for our project,' said Jo. 'Claire said we have to read everything we can.'

'Oh! Claire said. I might have known it was Claire! She seems to lay down the law rather a lot, doesn't she?'

Jo wrinkled her forehead beneath her fringe. 'Not really. It's just that she knows about ballet and I don't.'

'So why are you doing a project on something you don't know about?'

'Well, because that's the idea of it . . . so that you find out.'

'But you've just told me that Claire already knows!'

'Yes. Well. I mean – she'll find out things as well.'

'Oh, will she? I suppose the project was her idea and you just went along with it.'

Jo felt like saying, 'Well, Matty's going and doing one with Julie-Ann!' but pride wouldn't let her. She tilted her chin, flicking her hair back out of her eyes. 'I wanted to do it.'

'Hm.' Mrs Jameson sounded slightly sceptical.

'I *did*,' said Jo.

'All right, I'll believe you. Thousands wouldn't. Remind me, by the way, to take you into town next Saturday and get that hair cut, it's far too long.'

'No, it's not! I'm growing it.' Her aim was to be able to wear it in a pony tail like Claire's. If she scraped it back hard enough and secured the odd bits with hair grips she could just about manage to get it into an elastic band.

'You grew it once before, if you remember,' said Mrs Jameson, 'and you didn't like it.'

'It's different now. I've got to have it long, if I'm going to do ballet.'

'*If*,' said Mrs Jameson. 'A lot could happen between now and Christmas . . . you might discover that the idol has feet of clay.'

'What idol?' said Jo. What was her mother talking about? 'I haven't made any idols.' She'd made a wooden beetle, in CDT – '*That's* useful,' had said Andy. 'A lot of things you can do with a wooden beetle' – but she hadn't made any idols.

'You might discover,' said Mrs Jameson, 'that Claire isn't quite as wonderful as you think.'

'I don't think she's wonderful! It's just that we're doing this project together, and as a matter of fact she's asked me if I'd like to go to her place next Saturday and have tea and listen to her ballet records. Can I?'

'You seem to be seeing an awful lot of Claire just lately,' said Mrs Jameson. 'Whatever happened to Matty?'

Matty was going round with Julie-Ann. They were doing their project on slavery. Julie-Ann was now pretending – which Jo simply didn't *believe* – that her great-grandmother had been a slave. Some people would say anything for a bit of notoriety.

'Matty's working on her own project,' she said. 'And I *need* to listen to this music, I've got to write about it. So can I? Is it all right?'

'I suppose so,' said Mrs Jameson.

It would have been all right if Matty hadn't suddenly decided to go and have her birthday party on the same day. Originally she had been going to wait until half term, but Julie-Ann, as she explained while they waited at the bus stop together, was going to be away then and naturally she couldn't have a party without Julie-Ann, so now she was going to have it this Saturday instead.

'This Saturday's no good!' wailed Jo. 'I've already said that I'd go round to Claire's!'

Matty pursed her lips. She didn't actually say 'Too bad' but Jo felt it was what she was thinking.

'You should have told me earlier!'

'Didn't know earlier,' said Matty, 'did I?'

So all because of Julie-Ann, Jo was expected to change her plans. She kicked moodily at a piece of broken kerb stone and nearly shattered her big toe. Matty watched, stony faced.

'Who else is coming, anyway?'

Matty said that Nadge would be coming, and Lee Powell, and the rest of their lot, and Miles of course would be there, and Matty's cousins, who were both boys and had to come to keep Miles company, and Miles was going to ask Tom, who was bound to say yes because Tom could never resist an invitation if it meant things to eat, and if Tom were going to be there then Jo really *ought* to, but naturally if she thought it was more important to go round to Claire's then she must go round to Claire's. Matty would perfectly understand.

What Matty was really saying, under the pretence of not caring one way or the other, was that never before, since coming to Petersham, had she had a birthday party without Jo being present. But she's putting Julie-Ann before *me*, thought Jo.

A solution came to her: 'You could always invite Claire!'

Matty said she didn't want to invite Claire. She said it was her party and she didn't see why she should be expected to invite people she didn't like.

'But you've hardly invited *any*one from our class,' said Jo. 'Just me and Nadge and Jool. What about Barge and her lot? What about Trish and Laura?'

'I can't invite everyone,' said Matty, 'can I? My dad's going to take us to MacDonald's . . . just about break him, wouldn't it, if I invited everybody?'

Jo hadn't suggested she should invite everybody; just Trish and Laura and some of the people from their own class. Why go and invite Lee Powell and that mob when she could be inviting Barge and Bozzy and Fij? She put it to Matty but Matty just set her lips in stubborn fashion and said again that it was 'my party . . . when you have yours you can invite who you like.'

One lunch time the Nelligan Under-13s had a match against Sutton's, which they won by 17 goals to 12. Elizabeth Grey congratulated them afterwards, singling out Jo for special praise: 'You're coming on in leaps and bounds. Your game's improved enormously since the beginning of term. Keep it up, and who knows?'

'Who knows what?' wondered Jo, walking back with Fij across the Field.

'Who knows anything,' said Fij.

Jo pondered this cryptic utterance a while; then: 'You don't think she was going to chuck me out and now she isn't?'

'Could be,' said Fij.

'Or do you think' – Jo hesitated before saying it: the enormity of it brought a blush to her cheek – 'do you think she thinks I might stand a chance of making the school team?'

Fij looked at her, rather hard. Jo's blush deepened.

'I mean, of course, I'm only *speculating*.'

'So I should hope,' said Fij. Of all the Laing Gang, Fij was the most broad-minded when it came to other people's shortcomings – 'One has to accept, I suppose, that a person can't *help* being thoroughly objectionable and squirm-making and a complete irritation' – but not even Fij was prepared to tolerate arrogance and presumption on the part of a new girl. '*Nadge* will get into the team because Nadge has been trained in the way that we do things.'

'So have you,' said Jo, eager to make up for her lapse.

'Well, that is true,' agreed Fij. She preened for a moment. 'But so have lots of others, such as Lee, for example. She is *bound* to get a place. All I'm saying is that it's practically unheard of for a new girl to come waltzing in and just take over.'

Humbly Jo said: 'Perhaps I oughtn't even to try?'

'Oh, you might as well *try*,' said Fij, generous again

now that she had reduced Jo to her proper place. 'Nobody would blame you for *trying*.'

The trials were held next day after school. Matty said she was crazy: 'You'll never get in, and if you do you'll spend the whole of your life just playing netball . . . they have matches on *Saturdays*. You're *crazy*.'

She didn't say that Nadge was crazy. She just said, 'Oh, well, *Nadge*,' in tones that indicated Nadge was someone special and different and not to be governed by the rules which governed other people.

Jo wasn't really expecting to get into the school Under-13s but still she couldn't resist sidling down to the notice board first thing the following morning to sneak a look, just in case. Others were there before her – Jan Hammond and Katy Wells, amongst them – so she hummed a little song to herself, busy and important, and frowningly scanned the notice board as if in search of something quite other than netball, such as CLASSES IN DRIED FLOWER ARRANGEMENT.

'If you're looking to see if you're in the team,' said Katy, 'nobody is from your lot' (by 'your lot' she meant the whole of the first year) 'except Nadia Foster and Lee Powell.'

Jo's heart went thudding down into her nether regions. You couldn't *help* being disappointed, even though you'd known you didn't stand a chance.

'Two out of seven!' marvelled Jan. 'Only *two* – out of *seven*. And there are simply *dozens* of them! Dozens and *dozens*. How many of us are still young enough to qualify? Ten? And how many of us have got in?'

'Five,' said Katy. 'And *one* of us is team captain.'

'Well! It just goes to show,' said Jan, 'doesn't it?'

By now Jo had recovered sufficiently to risk a quick look.

'And I *said*,' reported Jo exultantly to Fij, a few minutes later, in 1N's form room, 'I said fancy that! I said. And you two are only reserves! I would have thought, I said, that being so much more *experienced* than the rest of us you would have been bound to be in the team.'

'What did they say?' said Fij.

'Oh! They didn't say anything. Just looked as if they'd like to stick pins in me and sort of huffed and puffed a bit and then flounced off.'

'They're probably making wax images even now,' said Fij.

Jo still hadn't made up her mind about Matty's birthday party. There were moments – such as when Matty was nice about her not getting into the netball team and generously refrained from saying 'I told you so' – when she thought that of course she must go; and then there were other moments, like Matty sitting next to Julie-Ann on the bus yet *again*, leaving Jo to stand, all by herself, when she thought that wild horses wouldn't drag her to the beastly thing. It was Mrs Jameson who finally made the decision for her.

'Jo, have you replied to Matty's invitation yet?' she said.

'Not yet,' said Jo.

'Well, isn't it about time you did? It does say RSVP, and I suppose you've done enough French by now to know what that means?'

'Ask Tom,' said Jo, cheekily. 'He's the expert.'

'*I* know what it means.' Tom puffed himself up. 'Means risspondy sill voo play.'

'*Respondez s'il vous plaît*; quite. Reply if you please. I think you'd better do so immediately.'

'I have,' said Tom.

'I know *you* have, I'm talking about Jo. They obviously take it for granted that you'll be going, but it's still bad manners not to reply.'

'I'm waiting to see,' said Jo.

'See what?'

'See if I want to.' It had been coming home on the bus that afternoon that Matty had gone and sat next to Julie-Ann. 'I've already told Claire I'd go round to her place.'

'Well, you'd better *un*tell her, then! I'm not having you desert Matty just because of this Claire. If you ask me, you're getting a bit silly and obsessed with Claire. All I ever seem to hear these days is *Claire says this* and *Claire says that*—'

'Got a crush on her,' said Tom.

'I have not!' Jo's cheeks fired up. 'And I'm *not* deserting Matty—'

She was about to say that Matty was deserting her, but her mother cut her short. 'You write a reply and you take it round there at once.'

'But I've already *told* Claire – I've already made all the arrangements. I arranged them *ages* before Matty arranged about her party. She's only having it on Saturday because of someone being away. I don't see why I should have to alter my plans just because she goes and alters hers.'

'I'll tell you why,' said Mrs Jameson. 'Because you were the one who let Matty down over the swimming. Remember? Now, you get and write that reply, I want to see it delivered before tea.'

When she told Claire, next day, that she wouldn't be able to go round on Saturday as planned, Claire looked quite blank. And then she said, 'Was it *this* Saturday?'

'Yes,' said Jo.

'Oh, well, that's all right,' said Claire. 'I thought it was next Saturday. Miss Lintott's taking me to the ballet this Saturday so I wouldn't have been there anyway.'

'So I'll come next Saturday, then, shall I?' said Jo.

It was a bit disconcerting that Claire had got the dates wrong – she *knew* it had been fixed for this Saturday – but it was good that she wasn't going to miss out.

9

Matty's party was perfectly horrid. Last year, when
Trish and Laura and the two Jos had been there, they
had played games. This year, when Jo suggested they
play something, Tom made a being-sick noise and Lee
Powell, in her aggressive way, said, 'Play what?'

Jo should have known better than to answer. She said,
'Well, we could play musical chairs, or . . . postman's
knock, or—'

'Kids' stuff!' shouted Lee.

Jo had a suspicion that in fact Julie-Ann and Matty
might rather have liked to play musical chairs, but of
course they couldn't admit it now. Who would be brave
enough to stand up and say they still enjoyed kids' stuff?
In any case, if Lee Powell didn't want to do something it
meant that nobody was allowed to do it, not even if it *was*
somebody else's party.

Going to MacDonald's was quite fun, though last year
there had been an iced birthday cake (a sponge one) and
sausage rolls and sandwiches, and bits of things on
sticks. Matty's mum knew all about Jo and her peculiar
tastes; she always made sure there was lots of stuff she
could eat. The only things she liked at MacDonald's
were the French fries. She really just picked at her
burger, though it wasn't a waste because Tom and Miles
shared it between them, so there wasn't the least need
for Lee to get all threatening about it and tell her that if

she were someone starving in Ethiopia she might not be 'quite so bleeding fussy'.

Tom, hatefully, said, 'She's always fussy. Just a way of gaining attention.'

Jo went bright scarlet. 'It's not!'

'So what is it, then?'

Tom looked at her, challengingly. She didn't know what to say. She could hardly say that she didn't *like* burgers or horrible gluggy milk shakes; not when Matty's dad had been generous enough to bring them all here. It was Matty's mum who came to her rescue. She said, 'You just leave your sister alone, young man! Some people happen to have more refined palates than others.'

'Couldn't afford a refined palate,' said Lee, 'if she was in Ethiopia.'

'Well, she's not in Ethiopia, so the question doesn't arise. If you're so worried about Ethiopia you should have brought a plastic bag and taken your meal back home to send to them.'

Lee muttered something about 'going all rotten by the time it got there' but at least she stopped attacking Jo.

When they got back to Matty's place they all sat round drinking Coke and watching a video of a film called *Who Framed Roger Rabbit?* It was a good film, but Jo found it difficult to concentrate because of all the noise going on. The noise was mainly caused by Nadge, screeching and giggling and scrambling about over the furniture, pursued by Rory, who was the littler of Matty's two cousins. Rory was only nine, so probably couldn't be expected to know any better, but Nadge was eleven going on twelve and Jo didn't think it right that someone of her age should carry on like that. The trouble with

Nadge was that she just couldn't sit still for any length of time. It was the same at school: half way through a class she would start being disruptive and have to be sent outside to stand in the corridor (unless the teacher happened to be Miss Lloyd or Mrs Stanley, who simply told her curtly to 'Sit down, Nadia, and stop making a nuisance of yourself.')

After a bit, some of the others started joining in – notably *Tom*. Jo tried reprimanding him. In her best school teachery voice she said, 'Tom, you oughtn't to be climbing about over the furniture like that,' but Tom just stuck his fingers in the air and said, 'You stuff it, you!'

'Her and her refined palate,' jeered Lee.

Jo thought, when the video came to an end, that the party would be finished, but, 'What do you want to do now?' shrieked Matty, just as over-excited as everyone else. 'Shall I get out my camera and take pictures?'

'Better hadn't,' said Julie-Ann. 'Only get broken.'

At least Julie-Ann had *some* sense. Nadge and Tom were already over by the record player, choosing records to put on. They had the volume turned up so high that china ornaments on the mantelpiece began rattling. Tom knew perfectly well he wasn't supposed to play music at that volume, it would upset the neighbours. Mum was always telling him.

She went across and plucked urgently at his sleeve. 'Tom! You know what Mum says!'

'What does Mum say?' He roared it at her, rudely.

'The *music*,' hissed Jo.

'What about the music?'

'It's too loud!'

'Too loud, too loud!'

Nadge, jigging about at Tom's side, took up the chant: 'Too loud, too loud. . . .'

Tom leered at Jo. With careless finger, he flicked her fringe into the air. 'What's it to you, Squit Head?'

He probably hadn't meant it, but one of his fingers jabbed her in the eye. She blinked, furiously.

'You'll get into trouble!'

'Get into trouble, into trouble. . . .' Nadge began leaping, vigorously – boing! boing! boing! – as if she were on springs. As she leapt, she gave another turn to the knob which said VOLUME CONTROL. The music blared, louder than ever.

'Turn it down!' bellowed Jo, red-faced.

'Shan't!' Tom jeered, and went leaping off after Nadge. 'You go pickle yourself, walnut features!'

'Stupid old prune!' That was Lee, taking advantage. If Jo's own brother could be horrid to her, why shouldn't she? 'Strange how some people seem to get their kicks from going round ruining other people's fun.'

Jo *didn't* go round ruining people's fun. She liked music just as much as anyone. But Mum had told Tom time and again about not upsetting the neighbours. She looked round for Matty, thinking to enlist her help, but Matty was over in the corner with Julie-Ann. They were giggling and making eyes at Dillon, who was Rory's elder brother. Dillon was very handsome; all the girls went for him. But she had never expected Matty to do so. After all, he was her *cousin* – and Matty had never been one to go stupid over boys. Everybody, suddenly, seemed to have been infected by lunacy. Even Miles, who as a rule was rather quiet and serious, was jumping up and down in the middle of the room with a girl called Susie Fern. Susie Fern was one of Nadge's mob.

Everybody except Jo, and of course the four boys, belonged to the same crowd. How mean of Matty not to ask Trish and Laura! And hardly anybody from Nellie's. It was no wonder Jo was feeling out of things. Tom was as hateful as could be. He never took much notice of her at the best of times, but this evening he was being downright beastly. Just because he wanted to impress Nadge. Stupid creature!

Jo tried to curl her lip, scornfully, but it wouldn't curl. Instead, it started to quiver, and her eyes started to prick, and she turned and went rushing from the room. She wasn't staying here a moment longer! It was the most loathsome party she had ever been to. She wished she had never come.

Without even bothering to search for Matty's mum and say thank you for having me, she snatched her coat off the pile in the hall and raced out through the front door. She could hear the thudding and throbbing of the record player all the way down the path. She jolly well hoped they got into trouble. She had *told* them.

Indoors she found her parents watching television. Her dad said, 'Hallo! Party finished?'

'Not yet.'

'So what happened? Throw you out, did they? Rowdy behaviour? Been beating people up?'

Jo shook her head. 'Just came home.'

'Why's that?' Mrs Jameson held out a hand, over the back of the sofa. 'Tired?'

'Didn't like it.'

'That doesn't sound like you!'

'They're playing music very *loud*,' said Jo. 'I told them they shouldn't, I said it would upset people, but they wouldn't listen, and Tom is just so *rude*.'

92

'Is he?' Mrs Jameson smiled, sympathetically. 'Brothers can be, at times.'

'Whereas sisters, of course,' said Mr Jameson, '*never* are.'

'Well, I wasn't! I just told him what Mum always says, about not upsetting the neighbours.' At that moment there was a sudden break in the sound coming from the television: quite clearly, from next door, could be heard the thundering beat of the music. 'You see?' cried Jo. 'They're still doing it! I told Tom you'd be mad at him and he just told me to go and pickle myself.'

'That *is* rude,' agreed Mrs Jameson.

'So will you be mad at him?'

'I shall certainly suggest he tries to be a bit more polite in the future.'

'No! I mean about playing the music?'

'Oh. Well – I suppose, just for once – in the circumstances . . . after all, it is a party. It's not the sort of thing that happens every day of the week, is it? I think one has to be prepared to make allowances *some*times.'

She wasn't even going to get mad at him.

On Friday, in the lunch hour, there was a special rehearsal for the *Dream* – 'Fairies only'.

'Today,' said Wendy, all bright and happy, 'we're going to do some singing.'

Gloom, instantly, descended: they had been doing their best to forget about the singing. Only the second years, who as a rule nursed vipers in their bosoms on account of being relegated to mere attendants instead of proper fairies with names, greeted the news with any degree of enthusiasm.

'*Now* we shall see,' said Katy Wells.

'*Shan't* we just!'

The second years visibly preened in anticipation. Jo, sandwiched between Melanie, with her flute-like trilling, and Fij with her off-key warble, wondered if she could get away with just mouthing the words. Bozzy said defiantly, 'I never *said* I could sing.'

'Don't worry about it, Chloë! I'm not looking for perfection.'

'Just as well,' sniggered Katy, 'in the circumstances!'

The singing was not a success. The second years carolled valiantly but were no match for Barge's loud and tuneless bellow. ('Wasn't going to let *them* get away with it,' she said, afterwards.) Wendy was doubled up on her chair, heaving. She had a handkerchief pressed to her mouth and seemed to be having some kind of seizure.

'Felicity,' she gasped, when at last she was able to speak, 'can it be that you are actually *tone deaf*?'

Much amused tittering from the second years. The first years bristled. Who did Wendy think she was, bringing them here only to insult them? Fij, with immense dignity, said: 'I was not aware of any deficiency but possibly some people have cloth ears.'

The second years fell about.

'I like it!' said Wendy. 'I like it! And Jo, that was perfectly splendid! A real piece of inventiveness – you looked as if you were in *agony*. All that effort, and not a sound to be heard!'

Jo felt her cheeks burning bright beneath her freckles. How had Wendy known she wasn't really singing? She wasn't supposed to have noticed!

'I do have a bit of a sore throat,' she said.

'Don't apologise! That's quite all right, you just keep it that way.'

'You mean' – Jo said it doubtfully – 'you mean, I don't have to sing?'

'No! You can be a miming fairy. And Margery, let's move you into the middle of the back row – and you two, Chloë and Felicity, you move apart slightly so that there's a gap . . . that's it! Now we can all have a good view of Margery and get the full benefit of what she's doing.'

The second years fell silent; stunned, no doubt. The first years were a bit stunned, too. After all, who on earth would *want* to get the full benefit of what Barge was doing? Her voice was quite loud enough and unpleasant enough without being pushed into further prominence. Only Barge herself seemed to see nothing peculiar in the arrangement.

'It just shows,' she said, afterwards, 'that Wendy is not *completely* useless. I must admit I had my doubts before. But obviously she realizes that someone with a strong voice is needed to give you all some ballast.'

Even Fij and Bozzy found it hard to stomach. Only Big Lol said loyally that 'with Barge there to pull us together we'll be all right'.

'With Barge there to blast us *out*,' muttered Bozzy. 'I've practically lost the hearing in my left ear, just *standing* near her.'

'It seriously occurs to me,' confided Fij, later, to Jo, 'that Wendy is not in her right mind.'

The thought had already occurred to Jo, but now that she didn't have to sing it didn't bother her quite so much. As she said to Fij, 'It will be Barge who is mainly making a laughing stock of herself, not the rest of us.'

Fij agreed that that was a comfort.

10

Jo had quite forgotten that Friday was the start of half term.

'You doing anything?' said Matty.

'Doing something to-morrow . . . going round to Claire's.'

Matty said, '*Ugh*.' And then: 'I don't see what you see in her. Horrid stuck-up thing.'

Matty only said that because she resented Jo going round there and leaving her on her own. She bet if Julie-Ann had been available she wouldn't have cared tuppence.

'Claire's not stuck up,' said Jo. 'Not when you get to know her.'

'Got nothing to be stuck up *about*,' said Matty. 'Not as if she's anything special.'

'She can dance,' said Jo.

'So what? Doesn't make her any better than anyone else. Way she carries on you'd think she was the flaming Queen or something.'

Jo spent Saturday morning – most of it – up in her broom cupboard practising ballet steps. Secretly, from her local branch library, she had borrowed a book called *Ballet for Beginners* and was working her way through it.

It said in the book that 'due care must be exercised if bad habits are not to develop'. Exercising care did not come easily to Jo, who was by nature rather a hit-or-miss sort of person, but she thought of Claire, endlessly doing her pliés and her battements, and forced herself to make quite sure that each new step was right before going on to the next one. She had even unhooked the full-length mirror from the bathroom wall and carried it through to her bedroom. If she stood it on the bed and propped it up against the pillows she could just about manage to see most of herself and check that she wasn't doing anything wrong, such as bending forward at the waist or turning out from the feet instead of from the hips.

The latter, she knew, was very important. She had watched Claire, when Claire hadn't realized that she was watching her, standing with her feet stuck out at right angles to each other so that they formed a completely straight line. When Jo had tried it, up in her broom cupboard, she couldn't help noticing that her feet tended to roll over at the ankles. Claire's didn't do that, so it had to be wrong.

Another thing Claire could do, because she had done it in gym one day, not showing off, just without thinking, and that was pick up one of her feet by the instep and lift it right over her head – though with Claire it couldn't really be called anything as clumsy as *lifting*, her leg simply seemed to unfurl. Jo found that she could almost do it, except for the last few centimetres, when it felt as if her hip might be going to come right out of its socket.

When she went down for lunch only Tom and Mrs Jameson were there. Mr Jameson had to be in the shop all day on a Saturday, and Andy was doing his Saturday job in the local supermarket. Tom said, 'I'm going down the Youth Club tonight with your friend Nadge.'

The way he said it, he made it sound as though he were doing Nadge some kind of favour. Embarrassed, probably, at having to admit that he was going out with a *girl*. Jo wondered whether to say something sneery, which was what Tom would have done had it been the other way round. The only reason she didn't was that she couldn't immediately think of anything.

'You gonna be there?' said Tom.

Jo shook her head. 'I'm going round to Claire's for tea.'

'*Tea*? You mean—' Tom picked up an imaginary teacup, holding it delicately between finger and thumb, with his little finger stuck up in the air. 'Tea as in tea party?'

'*Tea*,' said Jo.

'As in bread-and-jam and pieces-of-cake.' Mrs Jameson slapped at Tom's hand. 'Stop trying to be so clever all the time! And while I'm on the subject . . . what was all this I heard about you being rude to your sister at Matty's birthday party?'

'*Me*?' Tom opened his eyes wide across the table. '*Rude*?'

'You were horrible,' said Jo.

'Who says?'

'I do! You were as rude as rude.'

'Well, if I was, you deserved it! At least I didn't go round trying to stop people having fun. Honestly, talk about a wet blanket, she didn't join in *any*thing. Just sat there in a corner looking like she had a mouthful of cold sick.'

'Shut up, you pig, I didn't!'

'Yes, you did! I was ashamed of you.'

'Well, and I was ashamed of you! Climbing about on the furniture—'

'Climbing about on the furniture!' Tom mimicked her, his voice high and shrill.

'You're an idiot!' screamed Jo.

'I'm an idiot!' screamed Tom.

Jo picked up the nearest object, which happened to be a table spoon, and threw it at him. Tom roared, dramatically.

'Heaven help us!' cried Mrs Jameson. 'Who'd have kids?'

It had been agreed, originally, that Jo should go round to Claire's at three o'clock. She had supposed they would still be expecting her at that time, but when she got to Turnpike Lane there was nobody there. She rang at the bell and even banged with the knocker, but nobody came to answer it.

She stood for a moment, wondering what could have gone wrong. Perhaps there had been a mistake again? Perhaps Claire had thought it was *four* o'clock and they were all in Sainsbury's buying things for tea? Jo decided that she would go and walk round for an hour and then come back.

An hour was a very long time to spend just walking around. She started by going in to the big toyshop in the centre of town called Playmates, but after she had been there for about ten minutes a shop assistant came up and asked her what she wanted, and she had to admit that she didn't want anything, she was just looking, whereupon the shop assistant went away and said something to another shop assistant and the other shop assistant came over and asked Jo where her mother was.

Jo said, 'She isn't anywhere . . . she's at home.'

'I see,' said the shop assistant. 'Well, you won't touch anything, will you?'

In the end it just got too embarrassing, she felt that everyone was looking at her, waiting for her to start touching – or, even worse, to start *shop*lifting – so she left Playmates and went to sit in the gardens instead, and watch the pigeons; but she had only been *there* for about ten minutes when horror of horrors she saw Tom coming down the steps, with Nadge. They were holding hands! Tom and Nadge, holding hands!

Jo jumped from her seat and ran. The last thing she wanted was to be seen by Tom.

She spent the rest of the time in the junior library, reading books. At least the librarian left her alone and didn't keep asking her what she wanted or where her mother was.

At four o'clock she went back to Turnpike Lane. Relief! She could hear footsteps coming along the passage.

It was Claire's father who opened the door. He was a small, roly poly, comfortingly ordinary sort of man with a bald head and little fat tummy.

'Hallo,' he said. 'And what can I do for you?'

Jo said, 'I've come to have tea with Claire.'

'Oh, dear,' he said. 'That's awkward. Both Claire and her mother are out. Gone gallivanting up to town . . . did they know you were coming?'

'Yes,' said Jo. She hadn't actually reminded Claire, she had just taken it for granted that if she had remembered, then so would Claire have done. She hadn't seen Claire yesterday after lunch, because Jo had had her *Dream* rehearsal and Claire had left by the time they finished: she had been given permission to have the afternoon off for an important dancing exam.

'Perhaps there's been some muddle over dates?' said Mr Kramer. 'What d'you reckon?'

Jo nodded, slowly, trying to swallow a lump in her throat.

100

'I daresay that's what it is. I expect one of you said one day and one of you thought it was another . . . don't you worry! When they get home I'll tear strips off 'em. Give 'em a right talking to. It's that Claire, that's who it is . . . goes round with blinkers, that girl. Doesn't know what day of the week it is. What's your name, luv?'

'Jo Jameson,' said Jo.

'And what's your telephone number?'

She gave it to him.

'All right,' said Mr Kramer. 'I'll tell them, don't you worry.'

Jo trailed her way back up through the market and into the High Street. The High Street was full of Saturday afternoon shoppers, all busy and pushing. She had to wait ages for a bus, and then it turned out it was only going to the Red Lion pub, so at the Red Lion she had to get off again and wait for another one, and by the time another one came it was almost five o'clock and she was feeling thoroughly cold and miserable. How horrid of Claire not to have remembered! She hadn't remembered last Saturday, either. And it *had* been last Saturday. It was Claire who'd got it wrong, not Jo.

Tom came to the door to let Jo in.

'What you doing here?' he said. He sounded quite aggressive – as if Jo had no right to be there.

'I live here,' said Jo. 'Or p'raps you hadn't noticed?'

'Don't you be smart with me,' said Tom, 'or I'll garrot you!' He lunged towards her, making squeezing motions with his hands. 'Twist your neck till your eyes pop out . . . thought you were going to stay and have tea?'

'Decided not to.'

'Why? Did you quarrel?' It was Tom's firm belief that girls spent all their time quarrelling. When Jo, once, had

101

retorted that boys seemed to spend all their time fighting, Tom had said that fighting was different. Fighting was a *sport*: quarrelling was a silly, niminy piminy, girlish sort of activity. 'Did you tear each other's hair out?'

'Did who tear each other's hair out?' said Mrs Jameson, coming through from the kitchen at that moment with a pot of tea. She didn't seem particularly surprised to see Jo back so soon.

'Her and Claire,' said Tom. 'They've had a quarrel.'

'I'm sure they haven't,' said Mrs Jameson.

'No, we jolly well haven't,' said Jo.

'So why didn't you stay and have tea?'

''Cause Claire had relations coming, so there!'

'So why'd she ask you to go round, then? If she had relations coming?'

''Cause she didn't know till the last minute!'

'What, you mean—'

'Tom,' said Mrs Jameson, 'just be quiet, do you mind? Your voice gets on a person's nerves. Sit down and have your tea. Jo?' Jo noticed that there were three places laid at table. Had her mother forgotten she was supposed to be eating at Claire's? 'What are you doing tonight?' said Mrs Jameson. 'Are you going to go to the Youth Club with Tom?'

Go to the Youth Club with Tom? Her mother must be joking! 'I wouldn't go *any*where with Tom . . . not if they paid me!'

'Wouldn't take you,' Said Tom. 'Who'd want a miseryguts like you around?'

'*Tom!*' Mrs Jameson rapped, sharply, on the table. 'Will you please stop needling your sister? Get on with your food, get yourself washed, and get out!'

'And good riddance!'

'Jo, be quiet! That was quite unnecessary. What applies to Tom,' said Mrs Jameson, 'applies equally to you . . . just get on with your tea and stop needling.'

Jo ate the rest of her meal in sullen silence. Tom, defiant, crammed his mouth with cake, turned up the television, conversed loudly over the top of it, spat cake crumbs across the table and stuck his elbow in the butter. It was a relief when at last he went upstairs to wash his hands: it was even more of a relief when he finally left the house. Mrs Jameson walked across and turned the television back down.

'I didn't mention it before,' she said, 'because I didn't think you'd want to discuss it in front of Tom, but Claire's mother rang just before you got in.'

'Oh?' Jo looked up, quickly, from the piece of cake she had been crumbling on her plate.

'She was ringing to apologize . . . it seems Claire had quite forgotten to tell her you were supposed to be going round there for tea.'

'Oh.' Jo bent her head again over her plate. How *could* Claire forget? That was *twice*.

'Her mother said she was all up in the air because of taking some exam, and they'd been in to town to get her some new ballet shoes. She said she's extremely sorry about it and she's invited you round there for Monday instead – if you want to go, that is.'

Was there really something in her mother's tone which said, 'I wouldn't, if I were you,' or was it only her imagination? Jo pushed her fringe out of her eyes.

'I s'pose I might as well,' she said.

'Well, it's up to you . . . if you're not seeing Matty?'

Jo shook her head. She didn't know what Matty was

103

doing, without Julie-Ann, but they hadn't made any arrangements.

'Jo—' Mrs Jameson reached out a hand across the table. 'Is something wrong between you and Matty? You don't seem to do things together like you used to – and you still haven't told me what happened at the party. I can't believe it was just Tom, misbehaving! You must be used to that by now. What was it, really, that upset you?'

Jo crumbled assiduously at her cake.

'She hardly invited anyone from our class, *or* Trish and Laura.'

'Didn't she? Who did she invite, then?'

'Just invited all her own friends.'

'You mean Matty's friends aren't your friends?'

'Not really.'

'Why's that?'

There was a pause. 'They're all black!' said Jo.

'Is that any reason why you shouldn't be friends with them?'

'They make me feel like an outsider.'

'I'm sure they don't mean to.'

Jo thrust out her lower lip. Nadge mightn't mean to, but Lee Powell certainly did. So did Julie-Ann, though for different reasons. Julie-Ann just wanted to grab Matty for herself.

'Tell me,' said Mrs Jameson. Gently she removed the plate of cake crumbs from Jo's busily kneading fingers. 'How many black girls were there in your class at Juniors?'

'Weren't any,' mumbled Jo.

'Apart from Matty, of course. . . .'

Silence, while the implications of this slowly filtered through to Jo's consciousness. She looked up at her mother, forehead wrinkled.

'You don't think, do you,' said Mrs Jameson, 'that maybe there were times when Matty felt like an outsider?'

It was a temptation to say no, of course not; how could she? Matty had been part of a gang – Matty, Jammy, Trish and Laura. There hadn't been anyone spiteful like Lee Powell; there hadn't been anyone trying to snatch Jo for herself and take her away from Matty. At any rate. . . .

'What do you think?' said Mrs Jameson.

Jo rubbed a finger across her forehead. She was suddenly remembering a time when Little Jo had had a party and had not invited Matty; and another time when Big Jo, thinking she was being funny, had called her 'frizz bonce' and everyone had laughed. Jo had laughed along with all the others. She had never really stopped to consider how Matty might have felt.

'I expect what it is,' said Mrs Jameson, 'I expect Matty's finding her feet in a new environment just as you are. And if *you* had a party and invited all *your* new friends she would feel just as left out as you did. Don't you think?'

'Maybe,' said Jo. She hadn't quite seen it like that. She supposed her mother could be right – but it still didn't make it any better.

11

Tea at Claire's turned out to be rather an ordeal. Not knowing about Jo's peculiar eating habits, Mrs Kramer had gone to a great deal of trouble to prepare all the foods that she hated most: peanut butter sandwiches, tinned pears with hazelnut ice cream, and a deep, dark fruit cake simply stuffed full of currants and covered all over in yucky yellow marzipan. Jo hardly knew how to get it down her. The peanut butter sandwiches tasted like sawdust mixed with engine oil, the tinned pears – all slippy and slimy – made her feel sick, and the fruit cake rolled itself into great claggy lumps inside her mouth.

Mrs Kramer, who looked like an older version of Claire, gone a bit plump – except that it wasn't possible to imagine Claire ever going plump – beamed approval as Jo chewed and swallowed, and swallowed again, and drank her milky tea and tried not to gag, because milky tea was something else that made her feel sick, except one had to have liquid of *some* kind. At home she usually drank fresh fruit juice or just plain water, but she hadn't quite liked to ask Mrs Kramer for anything different. In any case, Jo's mum always filtered her water or bought it in bottles from the supermarket. Mrs Kramer's might come straight out of the tap, and Jo had heard that if you drank water out of the tap it made you go funny. Tom said this was nonsense and just another of her stupid fads, and put his mouth under the tap and drank gallons,

106

in order to show her, and it was perfectly true that Tom hadn't *yet* gone green or had his hair fall out, but who knew what might not happen in the future? Besides, knowing Tom he'd only pretended to drink.

'Another slice of cake?' said Mrs Kramer, already prepared to hack off a chunk.

'No, thank you,' said Jo, hastily. 'That was lovely. I'm really full up.'

'I'm glad you enjoyed it. It's good to see someone with a nice healthy appetite. I'm afraid Claire's a bit of a picker.'

Claire hadn't eaten any of the food that was on the table. She had just had plain crackers with a smear of marge and a bunch of radishes. Jo wished that she could have had the same. Plain crackers and radishes were two of the things that she liked.

'Of course,' said Mrs Kramer, 'Claire does have to stay very slim for the ballet.'

'Too slim, if you ask me.' That was Claire's dad, all roly poly with his bald pink head. 'I like to see someone with a bit of flesh on them.'

Jo hoped he wasn't referring to *her*. 'A bit of flesh' meant 'a bit of fat', and Jo knew, because of the measurements they had taken for costumes, that she was almost exactly the same size as Claire.

'Nice little round face,' said Mr Kramer, nodding at Jo. (Not the least *idea* that he was insulting her.) 'If you were to ask me, I'd say our Claire was a bit on the skinny side.'

Claire didn't say anything. Jo had noticed that she didn't seem to pay very much attention to what either of her parents said.

'Claire's all right,' said her mother. 'You can't have little round ballet dancers.'

I'm not little and round, thought Jo; and she sat up very straight on her chair, with her head held high and her hands neatly folded in her lap, as she had seen Claire do.

'Ballet's a different world,' said Mrs Kramer, for Jo's benefit, in case Jo mightn't have realized. 'Different rules. They don't behave like the rest of us.'

After tea they listened to Claire's ballet records, and Jo read the backs of the record sleeves so that she could follow the story line. Now and again Claire would say, 'This is where she meets the prince' or 'this is the Fairy of the Crystal Fountain', and would do a few steps to demonstrate. Jo watched the steps and memorized them, so that she could try them out later in her broom cupboard. She wished she were the sort of person who was bold enough to jump up and do some demonstrating of her own. She was sure, if she did, that Mrs Kramer would say, 'Oh, so we have *another* little dancer!'

She knew she could do some of the steps as well as Claire. Not all of them, naturally, because she hadn't yet been taught; but the simpler ones, which she had already learnt from her Ballet for Beginners book. Someone like Barge wouldn't hesitate. Barge was always keen to push herself forward where she felt that she would shine, even when she was quite mistaken, as with the dreadful singing episode. Barge had not the least doubt that her loud, bawling, totally untuneful voice was what the audience would want to hear.

Jo wasn't as brave as that. What she wanted was for someone – like Claire's mother, for instance – to say, 'What about Jo? Doesn't she dance?' and then Jo would say, 'Well, I haven't actually been *taught*', and Mrs Kramer would say, 'Oh, never mind about that! Let's see what you can do.' And then Jo would get up and would surprise everyone by being very nearly – not quite, because that would be unrealistic, but very *nearly* – as good as Claire. And then at last Claire would notice and say, 'Look, mum, she's a natural! Jam, why don't *you* do ballet? You ought to come along and meet Miss Lintott!'

But Claire never noticed anything, and Mrs Kramer was too busy explaining to Jo that 'That was the piece she's just done for her exam . . . that was the dance she did at last year's show . . . that's a particularly difficult step, which not many people of Claire's age can master.'

Difficult, was it? Jo watched and memorized and determined to try it out.

After they had listened to most of the records – not all the way through, just selected bits from each one – Jo thought that perhaps she and Claire might go up to Claire's bedroom to be on their own, which was what she and Matty always did, but instead Mrs Kramer brought out a photograph album and started showing Jo all the pictures she had taken of Claire doing her ballet. Claire giggled and said, 'Poor old you!' but actually Jo quite enjoyed going through them with Mrs Kramer. Claire was one of those people it was always a pleasure to look at (unlike Jo herself, who always came out all peculiar and gnomelike in photographs), and she didn't really mind not going up to Claire's bedroom because it had to be said, you couldn't really sit down for a cosy gossip with Claire. You couldn't swop secrets with her as you could with Matty. All Claire ever talked about was ballet – which of course was as it should be. Jo knew that. You had to be really dedicated if you wanted to be a dancer.

'Why does Claire call you Jam?' said Mrs Kramer, as she closed the last page of the album.

'Everybody calls her that,' said Claire.

'Yes, but why?'

'I suppose,' said Jo, 'it's because my surname is Jameson.'

'Oh! Like mine, before I got married, used to be Weed . . . everyone called me Weedy!'

Mrs Kramer laughed, and Jo, politely, laughed with her.

'Wouldn't call you Weedy now,' said Mr Kramer.

Jo saw Claire's mum pull her stomach in. She was obviously sensitive about her plumpness. Perhaps, back in the days when she had been called Weedy, she had been as tiny as Claire.

'Does everybody have a nickname?' she asked Jo.

'Mm. . . .' Jo wrinkled her forehead, trying to think. 'Most people.'

'So what is Claire's?'

'Claire hasn't got one.' It was hard to think of a nickname you could give Claire. Barge sometimes referred to her as Snooty Drawers, but that was just being rude.

By the time they had finished looking at the photographs it was eight o'clock and Mrs Kramer said she thought it was time Claire went upstairs to have her bath and wash her hair 'ready for to-morrow'.

'Claire has a very special day to-morrow . . . Miss Lintott is taking her to a ballet festival down in Kent, where she's going to represent the school. I always think she does better for an early night when she has to perform next day.'

Jo wondered whether being part of a Greek frieze for

110

A Midsummer Night's Dream would be classed as a performance, or whether ordinary school things didn't count. She asked Claire while Mrs Kramer was fetching the car keys so that she could take Jo home, but Claire just smiled, as if the very idea of *A Midsummer Night's Dream* caused her secret amusement. Mrs Kramer, coming back in in time to catch the tail end of Jo's question, said, 'Claire is really only doing that as a favour to the school. She had to get permission from Miss Lintott.'

'Miss Lintott may come and watch,' said Claire.

'Miss Lintott? Whatever would she want to come for?'

'She says you never know where you might discover hidden talent.'

'Well!' Mrs Kramer laughed, and looked across at Jo as if inviting her to share the joke. 'I thought you told me it was like dancing with a herd of elephants?'

'Oh, that's the fairies!' said Claire. She giggled. '*They're* like a herd of elephants. The others aren't so bad – I mean, they are trained dancers. Sort of. There's one girl, Lucy Abbott . . . she's quite good, actually.'

What about *me*? thought Jo. How could even Claire fail to notice that she was in a different category from the rest of the elephants? At least, hopefully, Miss Lintott would notice. After all, Miss Lintott was coming specially to look for hidden talent.

The Kramers' car wasn't properly a car at all but a van with the words L. J. KRAMER: PAINTER AND DECORATOR painted on the side of it in bright green letters. Jo was used to vans because her dad had one which said PETER JAMESON: ANTIQUES. But Dad only used his for work, not for driving people round in. Jo felt a bit embarrassed, being taken home in

something which said painter and decorator and was all
filled up with ladders and buckets and pots of paint. She
hoped that Matty wouldn't see her.

On the way there, it was Mrs Kramer who did most of
the talking. Not that Jo was shy – Miss Drew, in Juniors,
had one asked her whether she kept a spare tongue in
her mouth 'to take over when the other gets tired' – but
Mrs Kramer didn't seem particularly interested in
having a conversation. She just seemed to want to talk.

'I'm so glad,' she said, 'that Claire has found a friend.
It's so difficult for a gifted child – being gifted somehow
seems to cut them off. People just don't understand . . .
the ballet is *so* demanding. I get worried about her,
sometimes, but there's no stopping her. If a child has a
vocation I believe there's only one thing you can do and
that's go along with it. We moved heaven and earth to
get her into Miss Lintott's. A very difficult woman, that
–wonderful teacher, of course; but touchy. Won't accept
anyone who's not prepared to devote themselves body
and soul. Well, you can understand it, but it's quite a
drain on the resources. Six lessons a week . . . they don't
come cheap, I can tell you.'

'I know,' said Jo. 'I wrote for the prospectus.'

'Well, I'm prepared to work my fingers to the bone for
her, if that's what she really wants. And I don't think
anyone could doubt that it is. We haven't pushed her.
I'm not one of those ballet mothers that you read about.
It was her own choice entirely . . . Mum, she said, I want
to be a ballet dancer, she said; and I knew that she meant
it.'

'I'm going to start ballet at Christmas,' said Jo.

'Claire started when she was ten. Went to see a
performance of *Swan Lake* and that was it. There was no

112

holding her. I think you can always tell when a child is serious.'

'I'm serious,' said Jo.

'Of course, you have to have the build for it. Claire was lucky there. What do the other girls at school think of her? Do they envy her?'

'Well—' Jo hesitated, uncertain how to reply.

'Some of them at her old school, I think they were a bit jealous. Because, you see, Claire is our only child and we're prepared to make whatever sacrifices are necessary for her. At the same time, I do want her to have a normal life as far as possible. That's why I'm so glad she's made friends with someone like you – someone nice and ordinary. A proper little schoolgirl.'

Jo wasn't sure that she liked being called a proper little schoolgirl. It seemed to imply that that was *all* she was – just a dim little untalented nobody the same as millions of others.

'It isn't easy for Claire,' said Mrs Kramer, 'mixing with ordinary people. She just doesn't have that much in common with them. Not that she thinks she's in any way better, or superior, but gifted people do tend to be very single-minded. Ballet is her whole life. It sets her apart. I know that that's the way it has to be, it isn't any use trying to force her into doing things against her will, but it is such a relief that she's found someone like you. You at least seem to understand her.'

'Maybe that's because I'm a bit like her?' ventured Jo.

'Like Claire? Oh, no!' Mrs Kramer laughed. 'You're not like Claire! Look at the way you tucked into that tea today . . . did my heart good to see it! You wouldn't get Claire eating like that. A few dry crackers, a bunch of radishes . . . Mum, she says, I've got to think of my figure. At twelve years old!' Mrs Kramer pulled the van to a halt outside Jo's front door. 'It's the fact you're not like Claire that makes me happy. I feel you'll do her a world of good. You must come round again, and next time we'll try doing something nice and normal that us ordinary folk can enjoy. We don't all want to hear nothing but ballet ballet ballet all the time, do we?'

'I don't mind,' said Jo. 'I like ballet.'

'Claire lives it,' said Mrs Kramer. 'That's the difference.'

12

The first thing that happened after half term was a form netball match against Roper's – class 1N versus class 1R – which Nelligan's lost by a disgraceful 15 goals to 5. Both Matty and the Mouse were away with colds, which meant that Geraldine Stubbs and Ashley Wilkerson had to take their place. Gerry Stubbs played conscientiously, just as she did everything: Ash was worse than useless. In the cloakroom, afterwards, the team held a frenzied post-mortem.

'It's that Claire,' said Bozzy. 'Nadge *begged* her to play, just this once, and she absolutely wouldn't.'

'*No* sense of loyalty,' fumed Barge.

'You would *think*,' said Fij, 'that being a new girl she would be only too flattered to be asked. Any *normal* person would consider it an honour.'

'She obviously is *not* normal,' said Barge. 'I've long suspected it.'

'So what do we do? Let her get away with it?'

'No! We show her that anti-social behaviour will not be tolerated.'

'How do we do that?' said Ash.

'Yes, how do we?'

'Well . . .' said Barge.

They waited.

'Since I am form captain,' said Gerry Stubbs, 'I think it should be for me to pronounce.'

115

'Go on, then,' said Barge. 'You pronounce.'

'Very well. What I think,' said Gerry, 'is that she should be brought to book.'

'Bought a book?' That was Bozzy. 'I'm not buying her any books! What's she want a book for?'

'Rule book?' said Fij.

'She can buy her own rotten rule books! Why should we h—'

'*In other words*,' said Gerry, 'I propose that we call a form meeting and see what she has to say.'

Nadge, who up until this point had been more preoccupied with swinging herself from one side of the cloakroom to the other by way of the hot water pipes than with taking any active part in the discussion, now called out that that wouldn't do any good, Claire would only say what she had already said. They tilted their heads up towards her.

'Which was what?' said Barge. 'Exactly?'

'Just said she'd got a ballet class.'

'She's always got ballet classes. I wouldn't have thought it would hurt to miss just *one*.'

''Cording to her' – Nadge's voice floated down to them from somewhere near the ceiling – 'she's not allowed. Has to have a class every day.'

'She can't even miss just *one*?'

'Not according to her.'

'That,' said Gerry Stubbs, 'is what I should call a slight touch of monomania.'

Barge stuffed her trainers into her locker and closed the door with a bang. 'You can call it what you like . . . flaming loopy is what I'd call it.'

'But not actually in*sane*,' said Bozzy. 'Least, not as far as we know. That means she can be held responsible for her actions, like when people murder people and chop their bodies up and send them through the post in parcels and the judge says they're legally just as sane as everybody else.'

They thought about this for a minute. It seemed a dubious concept.

'So what are we actually charging her with?' said Jo.

'Treason. It's like deserting in times of war . . . people have been done to *death*,' said Bozzy, 'for deserting in times of war.'

'It's what is known as putting one's own interests before those of one's country; or, in this case,' said Gerry, 'one's House.'

'Precisely! You should have informed her' – Barge looked up, into the gloom, attempting to locate Nadge – 'that it was her bounden duty.'

'I did,' said Nadge. 'Sort of.'

'So what did she say to that? Exactly?'

'Just said' – hand over hand went Nadge along the water pipe – 'that netball was only a game, and she didn't' – grab, snatch, it was a good thing Nadge was athletic – 'didn't see why it was so important.'

'But the *House*!' squeaked Ash. She seemed to have forgotten that a few days ago she had thought Claire so wonderful.

'I would have thought,' said Fij, in her most reasonable tones, 'that even a new girl ought to be able to see the importance of being loyal to one's House?'

'You did mention it, I suppose?'

They looked up accusingly at Nadge, small and spidery in the shadows.

'I said we needed the points,' said Nadge.

'And what did she say to that?'

'*Exactly*?'

Nadge waited until she had reached the safety of the lockers, lowered herself on to the top of them and bounded lightly down on to the floor. 'Said she didn't understand what all the fuss was about.'

'*Fuss*?'

A shocked silence fell over the group. Even Barge was stunned into momentary speechlessness.

'This is unbel*iev*able,' spluttered Bozzy.

'A *new* girl—'

'Having the *arrogance*—'

'Someone really ought to tell her,' said Gerry, 'that one does expect a *certain* level of co-operation. After all, man is not an island, as the poet John Donne has made abundantly clear – at any rate' (loftily) 'to those of us who are in the habit of reading poetry he has. I couldn't answer for the rest.'

'No, and since Claire is almost certainly as ignorant as anyone,' said Barge, 'though of course I am speaking *entirely* from my own observation, you may correct me if I am wrong, but I *think* one may safely assume she is next door to a cretin, in which case she probably imagines John Donne is some kind of a disc jockey. . . .' – here Barge gave a small sarcastic laugh, doubtless to disguise the fact that until a few seconds ago she herself had never even heard of John Donne – 'Well! Given all that, might I suggest you *also* inform her that whilst netball may be only a game, *ballet*' – Barge swelled, portentously – '*ballet* is only *dancing*.'

She looked triumphantly at Jo as she said it. They were all looking at Jo – all except Nadge. Nadge was the only one who didn't seem unduly bothered by the fact that they had lost to Roper's by 15 goals to 5 and that

Claire was putting personal interests before those of the House.

'I think that you should be the one who tells her,' said Fij. 'I mean, you are the one who sees most of her. And as one new girl to another. . . .'

It was what Claire's mother had said: they didn't understand. If you were going to be something special and demanding like a ballet dancer, you couldn't be expected to live a normal ordinary life the same as other people. Jo could see it; why couldn't they?

If Barge and the rest couldn't understand Claire's point of view, it had to be said that no more could Claire understand theirs, as Jo discovered when she finally tackled her about it, at the end of afternoon school on the following day. Claire listened gravely to all that she had to say. Claire was good at listening; she never interrupted or shouted over the top of you. It gave you the mistaken impression that you might be getting through to her.

'And so,' concluded Jo, at the end of several minutes' earnest explanation, 'they decided that I should be the one to come and speak to you. Being as we are both new. They didn't want you to feel,' said Jo, improvising rather, 'that you were being *got* at, in any way.'

'But why are they mad at me?' said Claire. She turned wide grey eyes in innocent mystification upon Jo. She obviously hadn't grasped a single *one* of the principles at stake.

'Well, because, you see . . .' – Jo said it patiently – 'because we lost the match. And if you'd been playing instead of Ash, we might have won it, or at any rate not lost quite so badly.'

'But I had a class,' said Claire. 'I told them.'

119

'Yes, of course, and they *quite* appreciate that, but they just had this feeling that perhaps, just for *once* . . . seeing as it's so important – I mean, it does all count when we have the interhouse rally. The number of matches we've won. The number of goals we've scored . . . p'raps Nadge didn't quite explain it properly?'

'She said it all went towards the final total.'

'That's right,' said Jo.

She waited a moment, expectantly. Surely now Claire would understand? Claire remained silent.

'It's a case of – well, of *loyalty*,' said Jo. 'To the House. It's important.'

Claire shook her pony tail.

'Everyone keeps saying that. They said it right at the beginning. It seems silly to me. After all, *I* didn't choose which house I was going to be in. Neither did they. Lots of people wanted to be in quite different houses.'

'Well – yes; I know. But once you *are* in. . . .'

There was a pause.

'It'd be like if you were dancing in a ballet,' said Jo, 'and one night you decided you'd got something better to do and so you didn't turn up and the person who had to take your place wasn't any good and it all fell to pieces.'

'But I never *had* a place,' said Claire. 'I told them, when they first asked me . . . I *said* I couldn't stay on after school.'

'Yes.' Jo sighed. There didn't seem any way of making Claire understand how much it meant to most people, scoring points for the House, winning shields and cups and trophies.

'I wouldn't ever drop out of something once I'd agreed,' said Claire. 'That's why I'm still going to do the

Greek dancing for Wendy, even though Miss Lintott thinks I probably shouldn't be.'

'Why does Miss Lintott think you shouldn't be?'

'Well, because of all the exams and everything.'

'But we don't have exams this term.'

'*Ballet* exams.'

'Oh.' Jo found that instead of turning right at the end of Shapcott Lane, as usual, to catch her bus home, she was still walking with Claire, in the opposite direction. 'Are you going for a class now?'

'Yes. I always go straight from school.'

'Can I come with you?' She knew where Miss Lintott's studio was from the prospectus. She could just as easily catch her bus from there. 'I wouldn't expect to come right in,' she said.

'Miss Lintott wouldn't let you, anyway. She never lets people watch classes.'

'Not ever?'

'Hardly ever. Only if she thinks it will do someone good to have an audience.'

'Have you ever had an audience?'

'Only when I'm on stage.'

Jo would have liked to ask Claire how many times she had been on stage, and where, and when, and what she had danced, but Claire was funny about things like that. She didn't mind talking about ballet in general, but she always clammed up when it came to talking about herself. (Unlike Melanie, who was only too willing.) She wasn't terribly good at talking about school, either; mainly because she never seemed to know very much about what was going on. It had taken her ages to learn people's names. One time Jo had said to her, 'You know that Michelle Wandres?' hoping to have a good long

121

moan about her and enlist Claire's support, and Claire had said, 'Who's Michelle Wandres?' and Jo had had to explain, 'She's that horrid thing from the sixth who laughed at Bozzy,' and even then Claire hadn't properly been able to remember.

Another time Jo had said, 'I think Elizabeth Grey is really nice, don't you?' and Claire hadn't even known who Elizabeth Grey was. *Everybody* knew Elizabeth. She was not only games captain and Wendy Armstrong's best friend, but one of the most popular girls in the sixth. Claire really did seem to exist in a world of her own.

Miss Lintott's studio was right in the very centre of town (which was probably one of the reasons for her classes being so expensive) above a beauty parlour in the shopping precinct. Jo watched, wistfully, as Claire disappeared through a door at the side. She had a quick, tantalizing glimpse of a narrow staircase, then the door closed, abruptly excluding Jo from the wonders which lay behind. At the top of the stairs . . . what? What would there be? A studio. Big, light, airy. Full-length mirrors. Barres. A piano. And Claire in her tights and her tunic doing her pliés, doing her battements, a million miles from the mundane affairs of school. She suddenly saw it as Claire saw it. What did it really matter, who won a silly netball match? Who won the interhouse rally? How small and unimportant it all seemed compared to the things that went on behind the closed door, up in Miss Lintott's studio.

Jo turned, and walked slowly out to the High Street for her bus. She wondered what it would be like, to be Claire. To have parents who were prepared to work their fingers to the bone and make whatever sacrifices were necessary. *Her* rotten mouldy old parents weren't ever likely to make any sacrifices. Even assuming that Miss Lintott would accept her as a pupil – because by Christmas she would be eleven years and ten months, which was a whole year and ten months older than Claire had been when she had started – they were still only thinking in terms of one class a week. One class a week! Claire had *six*. How was she ever going to be able to catch up?

On the bus were a whole load of beastly boys in purple uniform. Amongst them were Tom and Miles, Matty's brother. Miles, who was always polite, smiled and said hallo. Tom said. 'Wotcha, Snotball! Who was that you were with?'

How did Tom know that she had been with anyone? 'Have you been *spying*?' she said.

Tom grinned, 'Saw you from the top of the bus . . . who was it?'

'Claire.' Jo said it reluctantly. She could do without any of Tom's horridnesses just at the moment.

'Oh! So that was Claire, was it? The famous Claire.' Tom turned and jammed his elbow into Miles's ribs. 'You listening?' he said. 'That was *Claire*.'

Miles nodded, and pobbled his head up and down on the end of his neck, and seemed in some way embarrassed. Maybe he was just in pain from being jabbed in the ribs.

'Nothing to do with either of you,' said Jo, and she opened her school bag and took out a book to show that as far as she was concerned the conversation was now over. She never talked to Tom in public if she could possibly avoid it. He was so horribly rude.

Next day, over tea, Tom said: 'You know that Claire?' '*Claire*,' said Jo. 'Not *that* Claire.'

'*That* Claire,' said Tom. 'Miles has got a thing about her.'

Jo tossed her hair back, scornfully. 'How can he have? He only saw her for five seconds.'

'These things happen very quickly,' said Tom.

Stupid. Boys were so *stupid*. Even Miles.

'He wants me to ask you something.'

'What?'

'He wants me to ask you if you'll ask her if she'll go to the Youth Club with him on Friday.'

'Why can't he ask her himself?'

'Doesn't know her, does he? Anyway, he's shy. He says,' said Tom, 'that if you ask her and she says yes he'll stand you a Coke and a packet of crisps.'

'Oh, yes? When?'

'Friday. At the Youth Club.'

'Who said *I* was going to go?'

'Matty's coming,' said Tom.

'Well . . .' Jo thought about it. She wouldn't actually *mind* going to the Youth Club, especially if Matty were going to be there. And she quite liked Miles. He wasn't as loud and rebarbative as Tom. If Tom had wanted an introduction to Claire she wouldn't have done it for a hundred Cokes and a thousand packets of crisps; but as it was for Miles. . . .

'All right,' she said, 'I'll ask. But I don't expect she will.'

She was surprised when Claire said yes; she really hadn't thought that she would. But that was what was exciting about Claire: she wasn't boringly predictable like most people. Most people were the same day in, day out till you could scream. Claire was obviously what Jo's mum called a dark horse.

'It'll make Miles ever so happy,' said Jo.

Claire giggled. 'I don't know about Miles . . . it'll make my mum ever so happy.'

Jo decided she wouldn't tell Miles that Claire was only going along to please her mother. After all, it didn't really matter what her reason was; she was going, that was the main thing.

13

Jo had never been to the Youth Club before. Last term, at Juniors, she had been considered too young. 'It's not for *toddlers*,' Tom had said. He couldn't very well say she was too young now, seeing as Nadge was a whole month younger, but that didn't stop him making beastly brother-ish sort of remarks about her appearance.

'You're not going looking like *that*?'

'Like what?' said Jo.

'Like that!'

'What's wrong with like that?' demanded Mrs Jameson. 'I think she looks very nice.'

Jo's heart sank: if her mum thought she looked very nice then there had to be something wrong.

'With her hair all scraped back? And that dress thing?'

What a pig. Jo had spent *ages* upstairs in the bathroom, in front of the full-length mirror, deciding what to put on, doing things to her hair. With the aid of an elastic band and several hair slides she had finally managed to pull her hair back into a pony tail. It was, admittedly, a very *short* pony tail; but it was still a pony tail. And the dress had come from Young Look in the High Street. It had a bib front over a white blouse, with a full skirt looped up to show a frilly petticoat beneath. Jo had chosen it specially, when she had gone shopping with Mrs Jameson at half term. Claire had one very similar.

'Look at it!' Tom swished, irritably, at her pony tail. 'Like a bunch of old bristles!'

'I must confess I prefer it when it's loose,' agreed Mrs Jameson. 'In fact, *I* preferred it when it was shorter. But I really don't see what's wrong with the dress.'

'It's yucky,' said Tom. 'Like something out of Twee Tales for Teenies.'

Jo flushed, angrily. 'This is the latest fashion!'

'Doesn't suit you,' said Tom.

What did *he* know about it?

'Looks ridiculous.'

'Tom! I will not have you saying things like that about your sister. That's a lovely little dress and it suits her perfectly.'

Tom scowled. 'Well, if she's going like that she can go by herself. *I*'m not taking her.'

'You don't have to take me!' screamed Jo. 'I won't go at all!'

She flew out of the room and raced upstairs, two at a time, to the broom cupboard, her heart pounding and thudding in her chest. Tom was hateful! He was just so *hate*ful.

After a few seconds there was a knock at the door. Tom's voice said, 'C'n I come in?'

Jo kept her face buried in the pillows. Tom stood over her. She could feel him there, by the side of the bed, all stiff and awkward. He had obviously been sent upstairs to apologize.

'I'm sorry,' he said.

Jo sniffed.

'I am,' said Tom. 'Honest. I didn't meant to upset you . . . it's just that it makes you look so babyish!'

Jo sprang round. 'Babyish?'

127

'With your hair like that. . . .' Tom backed away, nervously. Jo had been known to pack a good punch before now.

'How old does it make me look?' Jo snatched at the mirror from the top of her dressing table. 'Go on! How old?'

Tom shuffled, uncomfortably. ''bout nine?'

Jo's face, round and befreckled, stared up at her from the mirror. It was true: she *did* look about nine.

'Oh, all right!' With one hand she flung the mirror away from her, while with the other she yanked the elastic band and the hair slides from her hair. What suited Claire did not, it seemed, suit Jo. 'I'll put something else on!'

'It's not that it isn't a *nice* dress,' said Tom. 'It *is* a nice dress. I think it's a smashing dress. I th—'

'Out!' screeched Jo. 'Get out!'

In the end she wore her jeans and a sweater. Mrs Jameson said it was a shame, she had looked so pretty in her dress, but Tom said the jeans were good – 'Make you look all butch.' As they left the house he whispered, 'They don't really . . . I was just saying it.'

'Needn't think *I* care,' said Jo.

Matty was wearing her school uniform but had threaded two rows of brightly coloured beads into her hair and put on some lipstick. Jo thought she looked really sophisticated, in spite of the navy skirt and the socks.

'I couldn't be bothered to change,' said Matty. 'I'm only going 'cause of him.' She jerked her head at Miles, so that her beads flew out round her face. 'He's scared he won't have anyone to talk to.'

'He'll have Claire,' said Jo. She wondered how Matty

felt about her own brother having a thing about someone she didn't like.

'You can't rely on *her*,' said Matty, scornfully. Needless to say, she had heard all about the disastrous netball match.

'I'm sure she'll come now that she's said she'll come.'

'Believe *that* when I see it,' said Matty.

Perhaps, thought Jo, nervously, they should have gone round to Claire's and collected her. She had suggested it, but Claire had said it was all right, she could find her own way.

When they reached the Youth Club, which was held in a hall attached to one of the local churches, and saw Claire climbing out of her dad's van, Jo was too relieved to feel any embarrassment at the big green lettering on the side. (Even she, if the truth were known, had had a few secret niggling doubts as to Claire's reliability.) Tom, at the sight of her, strutted and puffed out his chest.

'Aren't you going to introduce us, then?'

'This is my brother Tom,' said Jo, 'and this is Miles.'

Miles hung back, and was shy. It was Tom who took charge, leading the way into the hall, showing them where they could leave their coats and 'doll themselves up'. Claire giggled at that and said, 'My mum's always saying she's going to doll herself up.'

'My mum says tart,' said Tom, 'but that's not a word I'd use in mixed company.'

Claire giggled again. 'Why not? Is it rude?'

'It means' – Tom made an elaborate pretence of looking over both shoulders to make sure no one was listening who shouldn't be – 'It means *prostitute*.'

Claire's grey eyes widened, gratifyingly. 'So why does your mum want to make herself look like a prostitute?'

129

'That,' said Tom, tapping the side of his nose, 'is the ten thousand dollar question.'

Tom was showing off. It was really rather disgusting. Of *course* Mrs Jameson didn't make herself look like a prostitute; he had absolutely no right to say that she did, and Claire oughtn't to be encouraging him.

'Let's go and take our coats off,' said Jo.

Claire followed her into the cloakroom. 'Your brother's funny,' she said.

'My brother is a pain,' said Jo.

'Yes, and he's going out with Nadge,' added Matty, but Claire was busy removing her coat and didn't hear.

Under her coat she was wearing the dress that was similar to Jo's. It was blue instead of pink and the bib had straps which crossed over at the back and fastened on to the waist band instead of tying round the neck as Jo's did, but otherwise it was really exactly the same. She wondered what Tom would say to *that*.

Claire, like Jo, had let her hair hang loose, so that it fell about her shoulders. Unlike Jo's it was very thick and blond and shiny, dead straight right until the last moment when it curled under at the edges of its own accord. You could tell it hadn't been permed or put in rollers. Jo wished that she could have hair like that. Her own was somewhat fluffy and ill-disciplined. Last year she had desperately wished that it were curly, like Matty's, so that she could do interesting things with it; now she thought she would rather have it straight, like Claire's.

When they came out of the cloakroom she saw that Nadge was already there – and so was Julie-Ann. Matty hadn't told Jo that Julie-Ann was coming. She attached herself to them immediately. She was looking as ludicrous as ever with with a big checked bow in her hair. Nadge, in white track suit and trainers, was playing table tennis with Tom. Jo looked round for Miles and saw him standing sheepishly in a corner with a group of other boys. She heard Julie-Ann say, 'Is Dee coming?' Dee was what they called Matty's cousin Dillon.

'I rang him,' said Matty. 'He said he might.'

So *that* explained why Matty had come (and why she had gone to all the trouble of threading beads in her hair.) Jo tossed her fringe out of her eyes.

'Let's go over and talk to Miles,' she said to Claire.

Miles seemed struck dumb by actually being in the presence of his beloved. If it hadn't been for Jo, prattling vigorously about just whatever came to her, they would all three have stood in silence, for Miles did nothing but make strangulated noises and keep swallowing at his Adam's apple while Claire contributed no more than the occasional vague smile. She might have given Jo *some* assistance – although, of course, Claire was never much of a talker, unless it was about ballet. Miles, on the other hand, was into astronomy in a big way. She didn't know whether Claire was interested in astronomy but it seemed unlikely. She probably knew as much about stars as Miles did about ballet, which was practically nothing. But Jo couldn't stand here all evening babbling and burbling. She decided that the best and kindest thing would be to leave them on their own, on the principle, as some people said about charity, that self-help was the *only* kind of help that was of any positive value. Miles rolled his eyes as she departed, and Claire made as if to follow.

'You stay here and talk to Miles,' said Jo. 'I'll go and. . . .' What? What was there to do in this place?

Nothing very much, from the looks of things. What did people normally do at youth clubs? She had thought it would be more interesting than this. 'I'll go and talk to Tom,' she said.

Tom was the last person she actually wanted to talk to but one had to do something, and she didn't know anyone else apart from Matty and Julie-Ann and they were hanging round the entrance waiting for Dillon. Serve them right if he didn't turn up. Probably wouldn't, if he knew they were lying in wait. Jo wouldn't have come if Matty had told her that Julie-Ann was going to be there. She had looked forward to having Matty to herself, like in the old days.

The Youth Club, she decided, wasn't really much of a youth club – just a big bare room with lots of tubular chairs all stacked on top of one another against the wall, and a piano, which was kept locked, at one end, with a couple of table tennis tables at the other. In one of the walls there was a serving hatch which gave on to a small kitchen, where Mrs Barlow, who was the mother of a girl called Angela Barlow who lived in the same road as Jo and Matty, kept a store of Cokes and crisps and popcorn. It was Mrs Barlow who really ran the Youth Club. Some nights she took them on special outings, or hired videos to show them, or organized discos, but tonight seemed to be a night for everyone doing what they wanted, which for the most part meant the girls standing round in little clumps, talking, and the boys running about shouting and kicking at one another.

Jo made her way across to the table where Tom and Nadge were playing table tennis. She stood for a moment, watching them, waiting for Tom to look up and see her and make one of his stupid showing-off type remarks, such as 'Here comes Poopy Face' or 'What's your problem, Squint Eye?' Instead, when at last he looked up at the end of a long rally – won by Nadge: she was glad Nadge was better than Tom at table tennis – he seemed to look straight through and beyond Jo, almost as if she had suddenly become transparent.

She turned, to see what had caught his attention, and found that Claire, in *spite* of her instructions to stay with Miles, had gone and followed her over. Jo felt cross. She felt how her mother must feel when she told them not to do certain things, like slamming their bedroom doors or putting their feet on the sofa, and then they went and did them.

Tom was staring, in a way that made him look distinctly foolish. His eyes had gone all bulgy and his mouth seemed as if it might be on the point of dropping open. It must be the dress, thought Jo; he probably thought it was the same one as she had been wearing. Apart from the colour they did look the same, and Tom could never tell, five minutes after seeing something, whether it had been blue or red or green. Privately Jo had a theory that he was colour blind and just didn't care to admit it.

'Tom,' she said, 'didn't anyone ever tell you it's very rude to stare?'

Tom started, and blushed. (*Tom*? *Blushing*? She had never seen that before.)

'D'you want to join in?' he said.

Jo opened her mouth to say no – for herself she wouldn't have minded: she was thinking of Miles – but already Tom was picking up a spare bat and handing it to Claire. (*Handing* it to her: not shoving it at her or chucking it at her, which were his normal ways of presenting people with things.)

'Me and Claire against Jo and Nadge . . . best of three!'

'But you hadn't finished your game,' protested Jo.

'Doesn't matter. Start a new one.'

She bet Nadge had been winning; she bet that was it. Tom couldn't stand to be beaten by a girl – 'specially one who was eighteen months younger than he was.

Jo had only ever played table tennis on the dining room table before and she didn't think Claire could ever have played at all, the way she kept serving everything straight into the net, but Nadge was good and Tom was slapdash and there wasn't any question of who the eventual winners would have been if they hadn't had to stop.

The reason they had to stop was that Mrs Barlow suddenly appeared and demanded everyone's attention. Tom, in his horrider moments, had sometimes said that Mrs Barlow was a daft old bat that nobody took any notice of, but everybody stopped all right when she clapped her hands so Jo reckoned she couldn't be as daft as all that.

'Now,' said Mrs Barlow, brightly, 'I thought that maybe tonight we would have a quiz.'

Groans from all parts of the room. Someone shouted, 'Not a *quiz*!'

All right, said Mrs Barlow, they wouldn't have a quiz. How about trying out some carols ready for the Christmas carol service?

More groans. 'We done that at school!'

Well, then, said Mrs Barlow, not quite so bright as she had been before, suppose they had a table tennis tournament?

'Not *again*!'

134

'We did that last month!'

Jo began to feel rather sorry for poor Mrs Barlow. She decided that when she was grown up one thing she would never do would be to organize a youth club. It seemed to her that people were most ungrateful.

'Very well, then,' said Mrs Barlow. She sounded slightly weary: Jo wasn't surprised. 'I shall go and open the snack bar and leave you to your own devices . . . and boys, please remember: *no fighting.*'

'Quick!' said Tom. He made a dive towards the table tennis tables. 'Let's get on with the game.'

Jo looked for Miles and saw him still standing in the same corner where he had been before.

'Shouldn't we let someone else have a go?' she said.

'Yeah, we should.' That was Nadge. Jo hadn't expected support from that quarter. Nadge was never happier than when she was playing something. 'Let's go and get a Coke.'

'In a minute,' said Tom. He picked up a bat and bounced a ball on the table. 'I want to finish this first.'

'But there's other people,' said Jo, thinking of Miles.

'Other people'll have to wait.'

'They've *been* waiting.'

'Too bad.' Tom slapped the ball hard with his bat so that it bounced up almost as high as the ceiling. 'First come, first served.'

'That's selfish!'

'Who cares?'

'Mum would,' said Jo.

Tom said nothing to this. With a self-satisfied smirk he caught the ball on its way back to earth and began bouncing it, up and down, on his bat.

'Well, *I*'m going to get a Coke.' Without looking

135

behind her to see whether Tom was following, Nadge turned abruptly and set off towards the bar, where Mrs Barlow was laying out her packets of crisps and popcorn.

Tom held out the bat to Claire. 'You'll play,' he said, 'won't you?'

'If you like,' said Claire.

'But—' Jo bit her lip. A fierce glare from Tom warned her to button it.

'You want to join in?' he said.

'No.'

'You mean, no *thank* you,' corrected Tom.

'I mean *no*,' said Jo.

'Suit yourself.'

Why was it that every single time she went anywhere with Tom they came to blows?

Jo moved away towards the bar, in search of Nadge. That was two people Tom had gone and upset – well, three if you included Jo herself, but she was only his sister so presumably didn't count. He seemed to feel he had every right to upset her. He had no right at *all* to go upsetting Miles and Nadge. Miles was one of his best mates and Nadge was *supposed* to be his girlfriend. People like Tom didn't deserve girlfriends if that was the way they were going to treat them.

By the time she reached the bar Nadge was no longer there: she had bought her Coke and gone off to join a group of boys who were kicking a football around. Jo admired Nadge for doing that. It was showing Tom that she didn't care, and it was a great pity, in Jo's opinion, that Miles couldn't do the same thing instead of hiding himself away looking all hangdog. He came over when he saw her standing at the bar.

'Would you like a Coke?' he said.

She let him buy it for her, and a packet of crisps, since it seemed to be what he wanted, though she did feel a bit guilty. Claire, after all, had hardly said two words to him since they had arrived.

'Tom is being so mean,' she said.

'That's all right,' said Miles.

He couldn't *really* think it was all right. He was just saying it because he didn't like unpleasantness. Well, Jo didn't like unpleasantness but if she were Miles she wouldn't just stand there. She would go over and do something.

'We could always go and join in,' she said. 'You could play with Claire and I could play with Tom.' She would, for Miles's sake, even though Tom was bound to yell at her every time she lost them a point. 'Shall we?'

'I'm not very good at table tennis,' said Miles.

'Well, neither am I,' said Jo. She wouldn't let *that* stop her.

Miles only shook his head and concentrated on squeezing his empty Coke can into an interesting shape. Poor Miles, thought Jo; he was really rather a *droopy* sort of person. He was nice, and he made you feel sorry for him, but he didn't have half the spirit that Nadge had.

14

On Saturday morning, Matty called round. The reason she *said* she had come was that she had left her maths book at school and wanted to borrow Jo's so that she could do her maths homework: the real reason was so they could talk about what had happened at the youth club.

'That Claire,' said Matty, sitting cross-legged on Jo's bed in the broom cupboard, 'she's nothing but a trouble-maker.'

'It wasn't Claire's fault,' said Jo, though in fact she couldn't help feeling Claire had been a bit thoughtless. After all, Jo had told her right at the beginning it was Miles who had wanted her to come. 'Tom was the one who was mostly to blame.'

'Yeah, but you didn't see her,' said Matty. 'You were over with Miles. I was right there, watching her.'

'So what did she do?'

'She *flirted*,' said Matty.

Jo frowned, and picked at a toenail through her sock. It was difficult to imagine Claire flirting – or at least, it was difficult to imagine her doing it *consciously*. She could see that to someone like Tom, who was obviously entering upon a silly phase (Andy had also been through a silly phase, but now thankfully seemed to have grown out of it) she could see that some of Claire's mannerisms might seem like encouragement. The way she would suddenly giggle, or give one of those slow, secretive smiles, or widen her big grey eyes; to Tom it would seem like a come-on, and to Matty it would look like deliberate flirting. What Tom and Matty didn't realize, not knowing Claire as Jo did, was that it wasn't intended to be either of those things. It was just Claire, being Claire. She couldn't help it if silly susceptible boys like Tom found her attractive.

'Even if she didn't fancy Miles,' said Matty, 'and there's no law says she has to, she must have known Tom was going with Nadge.'

'Not necessarily,' said Jo.

'She must've,' said Matty. 'Everybody does.'

Everybody might, but Claire wasn't everybody. She wasn't the same as the rest of them. She quite often didn't know the ordinary things that were going on all round her. She hadn't even noticed the time when Barge and Bozzy had had their row and threatened to punch each other's faces in. All the class had been talking about it, but when Jo had remarked to Claire, a day or so later, that 'Bozzy and Barge seem to be back together again', Claire hadn't realized they'd ever been apart.

She explained this to Matty, but Matty had already made up her mind. She wasn't going to listen to anything Jo had to say.

'She just better hadn't try anything on with Dee . . . she tries anything on with Dee I'll scratch her eyes out.'

'Seems funny you don't mind Jool doing it.' Jo had seen Julie-Ann simpering and niddy-nodding, trying to impress. Pathetic, if you asked her.

'Don't you get on Jool's case,' said Matty.

'Well, don't you get on Claire's! I don't mind if you want to go and scratch *Tom's* eyes out. You're quite welcome,' said Jo, 'to do that.'

'Tom's a boy,' said Matty. 'That's up to Miles.'

If it was up to Miles, then Tom would get away scot free. People like Tom took advantage of people like Miles.

Jo hadn't realized, until she arrived at school on Monday morning, how quickly news could spread. It seemed that the whole of 1N knew what had happened at the Youth Club on Friday and were up in arms about it.

As they took their places for the first class of the day, which was English with Miss Lloyd, Fij pushed a note in front of Jo. The note said, *Meeting in cloakroom at break. DO NOT TELL CK*, the last three words heavily underlined. Jo bet she knew who had organized it. She bet it was Barge. The Laing Gang liked nothing better than to hold secret meetings and plot things and plan things and get up campaigns against people who had crossed them. Fij and Bozzy just went along for the fun, and Big Lol was still at the stage of blindly following; it was Barge who was the prime mover.

Deliberately, Jo took out her Magic Marker and blodged it across the words until they had been completely blotted out. Fij, at her side, nodded approval. She thought that she was doing it to keep Claire from seeing, and knowing that there was going to be a meeting. In fact Jo was doing it to keep Claire from seeing and being hurt. She wouldn't betray them, though she did think, if they were going to accuse Claire of things, then really and truly it would only have been fair if Claire had been invited to be present. And what would she do at breaktime if it were one of those occasions when Claire sought her company? What excuse could she make? Jo wasn't very good at inventing things.

140

Fortunately there wasn't any need as Claire disappeared the minute the bell rang. The Nelligan first years, grim-faced, collected their breaktime buns and marched in a body down to the cloakrooms (where they weren't supposed to be, but as it was pouring with rain outside it was generally accepted that any prowling prefects, so long as they weren't Michelle Wandres, would turn a blind eye.)

'Right,' said Barge, *'if we are all here. . . .'*

Everyone was there save Claire and Nadge. Big Lol, who sat next to her, said that Nadge had had to go for a special netball practice with the school Under-13s.

'In the *rain*?'

'In the gym.'

'Oh. Well, in that case,' said Barge, 'we shall have to proceed without her, which may in any case be a bit more diplomatic' – *diplomatic*? *Barge*? – 'in view of the fact that what we are principally here to discuss is the perfectly disgraceful way in which she has been treated. Now, what I should propose—'

'Pardon me,' said Gerry Stubbs, 'but may I put a question?'

'Well, if you must.' Barge said it grudgingly. She hated interruptions. 'What is it?'

'I merely wished to refresh my memory,' said Gerry, 'as to which of us was voted form captain . . . was it you? Or was it me? I merely ask.'

'It was you,' piped the Mouse, helpfully. The Mouse was one of those people who didn't understand about sarcasm.

'Thank you so much,' said Gerry. 'I thought that it was, but the way things were going I couldn't be sure.'

'If you had waited' – Barge spoke with wounded

141

dignity – 'I was on the very point of handing over to you. But as you have premeditated me, you might as well get on with it.'

'Pre-empted,' said Gerry.

'You what?'

'Pre-empted, not premeditated.' Gerry hadn't been made form captain for nothing. It was a comfort, thought Jo, to know that they were in the hands of one who had so much learning.

In measured tones, Gerry laid forth the charges against the absent Claire:

'Inasmuch,' said Gerry, 'as she has repeatedly placed her personal interests above those of the form and of the house, not to mention the *school*; and inasmuch again as on Friday night just gone she quite deliberately set out to interpose herself between One of Us and Another Person, who shall be nameless but was in fact One of Us's boyfriend, as several witnesses here present will testify' – Gerry's eyes fixed for a moment upon Jo – 'this Court hereby accuses her of anti-social behaviour quite unacceptable in a civilized member of society.'

'Here here,' said Barge.

The Mouse, carried away, began clapping.

'So what happens now?' said Matty.

'Now we vote on it. Hands up everyone who finds the Prisoner guilty as charged?'

Silly idiots, thought Jo, as every hand except hers shot up. Claire was upstairs in the music room, practising the piano. How did they work out that she was their prisoner?

Gerry, frowning rather, said: 'Hands up all those who find the Prisoner *not* guilty as charged?'

Reluctantly, Jo's hand wavered into the air.

'State your case,' said Gerry.

This was horrible: everyone was looking at her.

'Well,' said Jo. She gulped, and tried again. 'The thing *is*, I don't think she deliberately did what you said . . . I don't think she realized that Tom belonged to Nadge. She doesn't always realize things. It's because of being single-minded and only thinking about ballet. Which is why, sometimes, she can seem a bit – um – well – different. From the rest of us. Like with the netball. She just doesn't understand,' said Jo.

There was a pause.

'If you don't shut up,' hissed Matty, 'you're going to make yourself unpopular.'

She probably already was. Barge was looking at her in a decidedly odd way.

'Do you wish to say anything more?' asked Gerry.

'Well – um – no,' said Jo. 'Not really. Except that when people are gifted they don't always see things quite the same way other people do and I think perhaps we have to be prepared to make – um – well – allowances. That's all.'

Jo had said everything she could think of to say. She hadn't wanted to say it, but she kept remembering Mrs Kramer and the talk that they had had in the car. Claire couldn't *help* being different. It was just the way she was.

Angry buzzings filled the cloakroom.

'Allowances!'

'*I* don't expect people to make allowances—'

'*No* kind of excuse.'

'And I am, I suppose—'

'*Thoroughly* anti-social!'

'–as gifted,' said Melanie, 'as anyone.' She looked

143

round, daring somebody to challenge her, but even Barge, for once, seemed prepared to let it pass.

Gerry banged on the floor.

'Silence in Court! We shall now deliver our verdict . . . the Prisoner has been found guilty as charged. And as I am form captain,' said Gerry, 'I shall decide what the sentence is to be.'

She sat for a moment, deliberating. Everyone watched, in respectful silence.

'All right,' said Gerry, 'I've decided . . . we've tried treating her like one of us and it hasn't worked. She's just flung it back in our faces—'

'Spat on us!'

'Treated us like *dirt*.'

'Silence in Court! Will members of the jury kindly not interrupt. The next person who interrupts,' said Gerry, 'gets done for contempt.'

Barge and Bozzy subsided, muttering.

'Thank you. I shall now resume. The Prisoner having been found guilty as charged, I hereby decree,' said Gerry, 'that no one is to talk to her from now until the end of term. By which time it is hoped she will have come to her senses and learnt to conduct herself more like a civilized human being.'

'After all,' said Fij, looking across rather anxiously at Jo, 'it's not as if we're not prepared to be tolerant.'

'Absolutely not,' said Barge. 'We simply ask that people should behave like people rather than expensive jars of marmalade.'

'Or Venus flytraps,' said Bozzy.

'Or Venus flytraps,' agreed Barge. 'One wouldn't have thought,' she said, 'that it was in any way an unreasonable sort of request. Please do correct me, anyone, if you think that I am wrong.'

Nobody did; not even Jo.

15

The trouble with sending someone like Claire to Coventry, as Barge somewhat peevishly observed, was that it involved a great deal of effort on the part of those who were doing the sending – having to remember all the time that they were not supposed to be on speaking terms – and no effort whatsoever on the part of the person who was being sent there; especially, as in this case, when that person seemed to have not the least idea that she was being studiously ignored and just carried on about her normal everyday business as if nothing were any different from how it had been before.

This was a particular source of annoyance to people such as Barge and Bozzy, who never objected to making these kind of self-sacrificing efforts for the public good but did expect to see some results.

'Do you suppose,' said Bozzy, after she had just pointedly ignored Claire for at least the sixth time that morning, 'do you suppose she has even *noticed* that we aren't speaking to her?'

There did seem to be some doubt in the matter.

'It's so hard to tell,' said Fij, 'when she never talks to anybody anyway.'

Barge, who shared a desk with Claire, said that she had twice-on-purpose leaned across her 'in the rudest way possible' to address a remark to Fij, 'and she never so much as batted an eyelid.'

It occurred to Jo that this was probably because such behaviour, coming from Barge, was nothing out of the ordinary, but she refrained from saying so. She was already under grave suspicion of having broken the rules by holding Unnecessary Converse. (Unnecessary Converse meant saying please or thank you when a simple snatch or shove would have been quite sufficient.) Barge had hinted darkly only yesterday that a Certain Person, 'whom I shall refrain from naming', might be sabotaging their efforts. It was Fij who had leapt to Jo's defence.

'I'm sure,' she had said, 'that we can safely trust *every*body in Nellie's to do what is right and proper and for the good of the House.'

It might have been more difficult for Jo if Claire had been around during breaktimes or the lunch hour. She wasn't sure, then, that she *could* have been trusted to do what was right and proper. Fortunately (since she had the feeling Barge would not be a good person to cross) temptation was largely removed by Claire spending most of her time up in the music rooms or attending rehearsals for the Greek frieze, while Jo was equally busy, what with netball and extra gym and the *Dream*, so that they were only really thrown together when they were working on their project. Even Barge accepted that you couldn't work on a project with someone without holding the occasional converse – 'But only so long as it's *necessary*.'

On Friday when they had had double art, and Jo and Claire had been sitting together copying ballet pictures from books they had borrowed from the library, Jo had been uncomfortably aware of Barge sitting directly behind her, straining her ears to catch any signs of unnecessary communication. Claire never had a great deal to say, so enforced silence didn't bother her – as Bozzy had speculated, she probably didn't even notice, being completely absorbed in her task of painting six rows of swans, all standing on tiptoe with their arms above their heads. Jo, wrestling unsuccessfully with a picture of a muscle-bound man doing the splits in mid-air, found it almost impossible not to chatter as she worked.

'Look at the mess I'm making . . . I just can't seem to get his legs right . . . look, it looks more like someone with two pairs of arms than someone doing the splits.'

Then Claire would be moved to inform her that the man wasn't doing the splits, that wasn't what it was called, and Jo would be on the point of opening her mouth to ask what it *was* called, when she would receive a warning kick from behind, accompanied by a loud throat clearing – 'Er-*hrrumph*!' – and guiltily she would press her lips tight shut and concentrate on making the legs look a bit more leglike and on *not holding Unnecessary Converse*.

Jo's problem, apart from the fact that she was a natural chatterbox, was that she felt guilty if she *did* hold unnecessary converse and guilty if she didn't. She could sympathize with the class for the way they felt, but she could also understand that Claire couldn't help being different, so that it really didn't seem fair to gang up against her. The only consolation was that Claire quite genuinely seemed not to realize.

A week before the dress rehearsal for *Midsummer Night's Dream* they had a costume call. The costumes had been designed by Michelle Wandres and made under her supervision by a team from the fourth and fifth years.

148

'They are not actually finished yet,' explained Michelle, 'so don't be alarmed if they don't quite fit properly . . . there are still some final touches to be added.'

Jo was glad she had said that, because the hem on her fairy costume was decidedly lopsided, and the circlet of flowers which she was supposed to wear on her head was so big that it fell right over her forehead and came to rest on top of her ears, forcing her to squint quite horribly in order to see anything. Melanie's costume had a long piece of gauze trailing from it, and Bozzy's was still held together by two large safety pins.

'Really, this is *most* unprofessional,' grumbled Melanie. 'It makes one wonder if they know what they are doing.'

'I know what I'm doing, thank you very much!' Michelle, in passing, slapped at Melanie's hand. 'Stop pulling at things!'

'But there is something *trailing*,' said Melanie.

'Don't worry about it.'

'Don't *worry* about it? When I could fall over and break my *neck*?'

'And what about my slippers?' Barge wanted to know.

Everyone else had been issued with real pink satin ballet shoes; only Barge was without.

'We'll find something,' said Michelle. 'A pair of hockey boots, or something.'

Michelle swept airily on her way. There was a moment's silence, then: '*Hockey* boots?' said Barge.

'I think perhaps it may have been her idea of a joke,' ventured Fij.

'Well, I should *hope* so! If they have run out of money, that's their concern, but I am certainly not going to appear on a public stage wearing a pair of *hockey* boots.'

'Of course you're not,' said Fij; but she didn't sound altogether certain.

'If you ask me,' said Melanie, 'Michelle Wandres is not quite right in the head.'

'Stark mad,' said Bozzy.

'Mad or malicious; one or the other. I begin to think,' said Melanie, 'that it may be deliberate malice.' She lowered her voice. 'Just *look* at what she has done to Oberon and Titania.'

They looked. Their mouths gaped open. Oberon had just appeared, clad from head to foot in bilious cabbage green.

'Like a stick insect,' marvelled Bozzy, 'on the point of being sick. . . .'

Behind Oberon lumbered Titania, in a billow of bright pink gauze. Even Bozzy was lost for words to describe it.

'Like a sort of – sort of. . . .'

Walking blancmange, thought Jo; only she didn't think it until some time later. At least, thank goodness, once the problems with hems and safety pins had been sorted out, the fairies were going to look presentable – well, fairies such as herself and Melanie were going to look presentable; she wasn't so sure about big, square fairies such as Barge, or big, fat fairies such as Lol, or even short stubby fairies and long thin fairies such as Bozzy and Fij. She really doubted whether white net party dresses with satin tops were altogether suitable when you were those sort of shapes. But then everyone had thought that certain people were decidedly odd choices for fairies in the first place, including some of those certain people themselves.

The main thing, decided Jo, pushing her circlet of flowers into a more becoming position on top of her head, was to make the most of oneself. She couldn't do much about the way the others looked, but she was jolly well going to make sure that *she* wasn't a laughing stock. After all, Miss Lintott was coming, in search of hidden talent. Jo secretly thought that with her crown properly fixed and her hem straightened out, and with her hair tied back into a neat ballet-type bun (it was just about long enough) she could hardly help but stand out from the others. Melanie might be prettier, but Melanie couldn't dance, whereas Jo had been practising the steps in the back garden every day for the past two weeks.

That evening her mother said, 'When is this display of yours taking place?'

'The Saturday before we break up,' said Jo, 'and it's not a display, it's Shakespeare, and it's all part of the interhouse competition.'

Every house was putting on one act of a play, or, in the case of *A Midsummer Night's Dream*, a selection of scenes from the play. York and Sutton were doing theirs on Saturday afternoon, Roper and Nelligan in the evening. There would then be a break for coffee, and after the break a panel of judges, appointed from the staff, would announce the winner and the runner-up. The points awarded would be added to the house total and carried forward to next term, and at the end of the school year the house with the most points would be awarded the Dorothy Beech Cup, which was a cup given by the parents of a distinguished Old Girl – Dorothy Beech – who had been killed driving ambulances in France in the First World War.

Each year's winner was inscribed on the big notice board in the main assembly hall, where it could be plainly seen that Nelligan had won far more times than anyone else. Unfortunately, that had been in the early years. For most of the past decade it had been Sutton's who had walked off with all the honours. It was one of the reasons that Barge and the rest were so furious with Claire: they had decreed that *this* year was to be the year that Nellie's made their come-back.

'Are we permitted to be present?' said Mr Jameson. 'Or is it a strictly inside job?'

'It's for everyone,' said Jo. 'Everyone that wants to come, can come. But you'll have to tell me quickly or there won't be any tickets.'

Mr and Mrs Jameson both said that they were going to come. Andy said that he thought he would, too – he'd heard there was 'lots of talent' in the sixth form at Peter's. He winked at Jo as he said it.

'Elizabeth Grey is good,' said Jo. 'She's playing one of the lovers . . . she's our games captain. She's super.'

Andy said that in that case he would definitely come, so that he could watch out for Elizabeth Grey. Tom wanted to know whether Claire was in it.

'She's part of the Greek frieze,' said Jo.

'Greek *freeze*?'

'Yes. Because of it being *Midsummer Night's Dream* and a wood outside Athens.'

Tom looked blank. 'So why is it freezing?'

'It's not *freezing*.'

'You just said—'

Andy gave a great guffaw. 'An fr-*I*-eze, you nit! Like a sort of decorative border.'

Tom scowled. He hated being made to look stupid.

'Anyway,' said Jo, 'I'd have thought you'd be more interested to know whether Nadge was in it.'

The scowl deepened. Tom knew very well how Jo felt

about the way he had treated Nadge. *And* Miles. He had shouted at her that it wasn't any of her business, but she could tell that he felt guilty.

'I think we'll all come along,' said Mrs Jameson. 'A bit of culture will do Thomas a world of good.'

Jo doubted that. She privately considered that Tom was beyond redemption.

The projects were finished and handed in. (Miss Lloyd said she would mark them over the Christmas holidays and hand them back next term: the best of them would then go on display for visitors to look at on Parents' Day.)

The Nelligan Under-13s played matches against Roper's and York's and won by comfortable margins, while the Nelligan first years soundly thrashed the Sutton mob, all of which so pleased Barge that she actually forgot she wasn't supposed to be on speaking terms with Claire and held Unnecessary Converse with her (on the subject of some French homework which Claire had done and Barge hadn't, and which Barge regarded it as her right to copy – on the principle of 'We in this House believe in *sharing*.') Once Barge had broken the barrier, others followed suit. As Fij said, 'We've achieved what we set out to achieve . . . we've shown her that she can't get away with anti-social behaviour.'

Claire seemed no more surprised by people suddenly talking to her again than she had by their suddenly stopping.

Trying to sound her out, Jo said: 'I expect you may have noticed things have been a bit quiet just lately.'

They were in the hall at the time, waiting for Wendy to

arrive for their last full rehearsal before the final Saturday run-through. Claire giggled and said, 'You mean the elephants haven't been dancing?'

Jo wondered whether to bother explaining what she had really meant and decided against it. Claire obviously *hadn't* noticed, and in the meanwhile, now that she was allowed to communicate again, there were far more important things to talk about, such as the vexed subject of the elephant parade, which was what people were starting to call it. Jo was anxious to dissociate herself.

'They *are* a bit heavy on their feet,' she said, 'aren't they? You can't imagine what it's like, having to dance with them.'

'*Dance*?' said Claire. She giggled. 'Is that what you call it?'

'Well, of course, I'm being kind,' said Jo. 'They can't help it, it's the way they're built. I really can't think why Wendy chose them.'

'I can,' said Claire. She giggled again. 'She obviously wanted a comedy show!'

Jo flushed but persevered. 'It makes it extremely difficult,' she said, 'for those of us that are of more normal proportions . . . getting *trodden* on by Bozzy and *poked* at by Fij and *trampled* over by Barge. Goodness knows what the audience are going to think.'

'I shouldn't worry about it,' said Claire, kindly. 'It's obviously not meant to be taken seriously or she'd have chosen proper dancers.'

'Yes, but for those of us that *can* dance—'

'They're very simple steps; they're the sort of thing Miss Lintott does with babies. I don't expect even Barge could get them very wrong.'

Simple? Jo had spent *hours* practising those steps.

'Even simple things,' she said, 'can either be done *with* style or *without*.'

'And the elephants are going to do it without!'

'*I'm* not,' said Jo. 'The others can do as they like.'

'It would be ever so funny if someone like Barge fell off the stage . . . I've told Miss Lintott about Barge. She says she's going to watch out for her.'

Watch out for *Barge*?

'And Lucy Abbott,' said Claire. 'Only for different reasons!'

Well, at least she knew for certain that Miss Lintott was going to be there. And if Miss Lintott were watching out for Barge she could hardly fail to notice Jo, considering Jo was the number one fairy who led all the others.

'Will she be staying on afterwards, do you think?'

'Who, Miss Lintott? I think she may stay and have a coffee. Why? Do you want to meet her?'

'*Could* I?'

'I expect so,' said Claire, carelessly, 'if I tell her you're my friend.'

16

Dress rehearsals for all four houses were to take place on Saturday morning. Every house had its own allotted rehearsal room – Sutton's in the big hall (because they were being ambitious and doing battle scenes from *Richard III*), York in the small hall, Roper's in the senior library and Nellie's in the gym.

One end of the gym had been screened off for use as a wardrobe area. When Jo arrived at ten o'clock, which was the time the fairies had been called, distinct sounds of panic and hysteria could already be heard issuing forth. She heard Barge's voice, bellowing above the others: '*Wellies*? Who ever heard of a fairy in *wellies*?'

Alarmed, Jo hastened round the screens. A horrid and ghastly sight met her eyes: Barge, in a froth of white gauze, with her feet solidly planted in a pair of big green Wellingtons. Jo had to stifle an impulse to giggle. Barge looked *ridiculous*.

Barge was not the only one. Around her, in varying states of outrage, stood Fij, drooping, with a broken wand: Bozzy, still with her safety pins, and her tights all round her ankles: Melanie, trailing yards of hem, and Katy Wells with a pair of big pink specs perched on her nose. They looked like an assortment of garden gnomes being sold off cheap because they had gone wrong. This time, Jo did giggle. She couldn't help it. Melanie turned on her, rather frostily.

'If you think this is amusing,' she said, 'just wait till you see what *you* look like.'

Her words had the desired effect: Jo sobered up at once.

'Where's Peaseblossom? Are you Peaseblossom?' Michelle Wandres grabbed hold of her. 'Come and get into your gear.'

Apprehensively, Jo allowed herself to be yanked over to the rack where the remaining fairy costumes were hanging.

'Here you are.' Michelle thrust a hanger at her. 'This is yours. And you lot over there, you can just shut up! *I*'m the designer, *I* say what you shall wear.'

'But *glasses*.' Katy spoke bitterly: glasses were the ultimate humiliation. 'Nobody wears *glasses* with a *crown*.'

'Why not? The Queen does. Anyway, it's not a crown, it's more like a sort of tiara. Felicity, what are you doing with that wand?'

'I am attempting,' said Fij, with dignity, 'to lash it together with a round turn and two half hitches.'

'Well, don't!'

'But it's *broken*,' said Fij.

'I'm aware that it's broken. It was made that way – it's the way that I want it.'

'You want it *broken*?'

'That is how I designed it, therefore that is how I want it.'

'I suppose next she will say,' hissed Bozzy, rather too audibly to Barge, 'that she designed my costume to have safety pins.'

'Yes, I did!' Michelle spun round, sharply. 'You weren't *presuming*, I hope, that it was shoddy workmanship?'

Bozzy, disconcerted, plucked at her oversize tights. (She kept trying to haul them up round her waist, but they kept descending again, gathering in big baggy pleats about her ankles.)

'Excuse our ignorance.' Barge said it witheringly. 'We rather imagined you must have run out of money. It is the only charitable explanation we could think of.'

'That just shows what sordid little minds you all have. Money has absolutely nothing to do with it. This,' said Michelle, waving a lordly hand at the wellies and the safety pins, the broken wand, the pink specs, the trailing gauze, 'is all part of the overall plan.'

'Oh, really?' blustered Barge. To Bozzy, under her breath, she muttered, 'Could have fooled *me*.'

'I evidently did.' Michelle retorted it, crushingly. 'Come along, Peaseblossom, stop making heavy weather of things – and stop plucking at that tiara!' With both hands, she grabbed Jo's circlet of flowers and rammed it down over her forehead. '*That's* how it should be worn.'

'Oh, my goodness!' Melanie put a hand to her mouth and tittered. 'Pardon me, but I have to laugh.'

Everyone turned, eagerly. Jo took a quick glance at herself in one of the full-length mirrors which had been brought down from the Home Ec. department and flushed a deep, resentful scarlet. She knew now how the others must have felt when she had giggled at them. The hem of her dress – her lovely white net dress with the satin top, in which she had fondly imagined herself looking like one of the swans out of *Swan Lake* – hung dismally down behind and looped ludicrously up in the front. Her circlet of flowers – so pretty, with its little pink rosebuds and dainty blue forget-me-nots – had come to

158

rest on top of her eyebrows, so that her fringe stuck out underneath like a scrubbing brush. One of the rosebuds had come adrift and was hanging down, rakishly, over her nose.

'That is absolutely splendid!' cried Michelle. 'Exactly what I wanted! It will be even better if you can keep on squinting!'

Jo didn't say anything. She couldn't: she felt too aghast.

'Do you mind my asking,' said Melanie, in a voice suddenly gone very quiet and quivering, 'if we are *meant* to be a laughing stock?'

'Well, we want people to laugh,' said Michelle, 'obviously.'

'Obviously?' said Melanie. Her voice rose, trembling, by half an octave.

'Put it this way' – carelessly, Michelle tugged at Bozzy's tights, rumpling them even further – 'there's not much point in having comic relief if nobody is going to find it funny. Is there?'

Pause.

'Did I hear someone say comic relief?' said Barge.

'I think Michelle may have done,' murmured Fij, sounding rather faint and far away.

'Comic *relief*?'

'I think so.'

'*Us*?'

'My dear girl' – Michelle sounded amused – 'you surely didn't imagine you were intended to be taken seriously?'

As Barge said afterwards, as they broke for lunch, it wouldn't have been so bad if someone had thought to *tell* them.

'I am as willing as anyone to do my bit, but if I am expected to stand up there and be pelted with rotten eggs I do think they should have had the graciousness to *warn* one.'

'I don't expect anybody will actually *pelt* us,' said Bozzy. 'Hopefully they will just stuff their handkerchieves into their mouths and think that we are being funny on purpose.'

'Well, now that I know,' said Barge, 'I naturally *shall* be. But how they expected one to be amusing when one was labouring under the illusion that a strong dramatic performance was called for is quite beyond me.'

The second years, whose morale had been considerably boosted – they understood now, they said, why all the main parts had been given to first years – ventured to suggest that quite possibly Barge might be at her comically most inspired precisely when she *was* labouring under the illusion that a strong dramatic performance was called for.

'I'm sure,' said Katy, 'that we have all found your antics over the past few weeks to be humour of the very *highest* order.'

'The funniest thing since Stanny stepped on a bit of old cabbage leaf and went waltzing the whole length of the corridor.'

'With one leg up in the air and her arms outstretched for balance.'

'Oh, we did laugh!'

'For all that,' said Katy, earnestly, 'I do believe Margery has been even funnier.'

'Yes, it would be a shame if she were to lose it now that she knows she is *supposed* to be.'

The second years reeled off, exceedingly pleased with

themselves, leaving behind a group of thoroughly demoralized first years. Not even Barge, purple in the face, could think of any satisfactory come-back.

'It is all so unpro*fessional*,' wailed Melanie.

'That lot always were.'

'I didn't mean them, I meant Wendy . . . not telling us. It alters one's whole *con*cept of the part.'

Jo, who was still in a state of shock, trailed dismally in the wake of the others, through the school gates and out into Shapcott Road. It had certainly altered her concept, all right. More than just altered: *shattered*. How could she hope to impress Miss Lintott as having hidden talent in a dress with a switchback hem and a flower dangling over the tip of her nose? She certainly wasn't going to add to the horrors by agreeing to Michelle's absurd request that she should squint. She didn't have to do what Michelle said. Michelle wasn't directing them, she was only the designer, and a jolly lousy designer at that. Fairies in Wellington boots! If Shakespeare had wanted fairies in boots he would have said so. *Enter fairies, in boots*. He was always doing that sort of thing. But in this case he hadn't, so he quite plainly wanted his fairies to be perfectly normal, ordinary fairies, which meant pretty and dainty.

'If the performance is anything like the dress rehearsal,' Fij was saying glumly, 'we shan't stand a chance.'

The dress rehearsal had been quite dreadful. *Twice* Bozzy had turned the wrong way and gone stomping off in a different direction from everyone else; Melanie had tripped over her trailing piece of gauze, Jo, unable to see straight because of her squashed down fringe, had blundered into Barge, who had stepped backwards and trodden on a second year in her Wellington boots, and Fij had forgotten her line – which, considering it consisted of only two words and had already been said once by Cobweb and once by Moth, was no inconsiderable feat. Fij, in defence, had claimed afterwards that she hadn't forgotten it, it was just that she had been distracted by the sight of the flower 'bobbling about over Jammy's nose and sort of *woffling* every time she breathed'.

To the first years' shame, Wendy had said that if the line were going to give her problems she had better work from a script, and had handed her a sheet of paper with the words 'And I' written on it. She had also removed the pink spectacles from Katy and given them to Fij to wear instead. Jo had been mortified to see Elizabeth Grey and another sixth former howling on each other's shoulders.

'But one has to remember,' said Barge, bitterly, 'that this would appear to be what they want.'

'And besides,' added Melanie, 'everybody knows that a bad dress rehearsal means a good performance.'

It was difficult, in the circumstances, to imagine what a good performance might be.

At home over lunch with Tom and her mother, trying desperately to sound casual, Jo said: 'Do you really want to come this afternoon?'

'I should say!' said Mrs Jameson. 'We're looking forward to it.'

'You don't think perhaps you might get bored?' said Jo.

'Certainly we shan't get bored.'

'But it goes on for *hours*.'

'Five-thirty till eight-thirty? I don't call that *hours*.'

162

'Yes, but then there's the judging, and then we have to go back and see who's won, and then—'

'And then we can come home and it will have been an extremely pleasant evening, far better than sitting in front of the television set.'

'But Tom *likes* sitting in front of the television set.'

'No, he doesn't!' shouted Tom. 'He likes coming to watch you make a spectacle of herself . . . you know her trouble, don't you?' He turned, triumphantly, to Mrs Jameson. 'Doesn't want us to see her all tarted up as a *fairy*!'

So long as they sat at the back and behaved themselves, which meant no whispering or passing of comments, members of casts were allowed in to the hall to watch rival performances. The Nelligan first years sat dutifully through battle scenes from *Richard III*, which included a girl from the sixth called Cynthia Rogers wearing black tights and a false nose with a pillow stuck up the back of her sweater to represent a hump, and bits of cardboard painted silver to represent armour, and yawningly through an act of *A Winter's Tale*, which was interminable and boring though '*Frightfully* good' and '*bound* to win first prize' as they all earnestly assured one another.

After the first interval there was an act of *Romeo & Juliet* from Roper's – 'Always so *gooey*,' complained Barge, who didn't go for romance – followed by Nelligan's with *A Midsummer Night's Dream*.

'Star billing,' gloated Melanie, as they changed into their costumes. 'It's always best to come on last.'

'Might be best to come *on* last,' said Bozzy. 'It certainly won't be best when we actually *come* last, which we are almost certain to do.'

'Not if I have my way.' Melanie seemed to have recovered her spirits after the depressing events of the morning. She sounded almost happy. 'I've been talking to my uncle' – groan from Barge, rolled eyes from Bozzy – 'and he says that since there is nothing we can do to alter the situation at this late stage our only hope is to go with it . . . he says that a true professional would never just sit back and moan. If you are clever enough you can turn almost any situation to your advantage.'

'I should like to know how,' said Barge, angrily, 'with your feet stuck in a pair of green Wellies!'

'I told him about that . . . he said the green Wellies would be a heaven-sent opportunity to any actor who had a spark of comedy about him.'

'Oh, did he? Well, ho hum *ha*,' said Barge, 'that's all *I* can say.'

'Who wants to be laughed at?' moaned Fij.

'I do!' With an air of triumph, Melanie suddenly spun round to face them: two rows of orange peel teeth protruded from her mouth. She beamed, fatuously, looking quite unlike her normal glamorous self. 'Go with it . . . that's what my uncle says!'

Once they had grasped the idea, there was no stopping them. By the time Michelle arrived to check their make-up, Fij had blacked out one of her front teeth, Bozzy had stuck two wads of cotton wool in her cheeks, making herself look like an amiable if slightly demented hamster, even the second years, not wishing to be left out of the fun, had given themselves an assortment of spots, scabs and pimples. Big Lol, who looked ridiculous enough in white net as it was, had gamely painted the end of her nose bright purple. Only Jo had made no concessions, considering that a switchback hem and a flower hanging over her nose were quite sufficient cause for mirth without adding to them. She was still not sure that she really wanted to be laughed at. It wasn't something she would normally have minded, but not if Miss Lintott were going to be out there, which she knew that she was for Claire had told her – 'Miss Lintott is sitting in the front row.'

Claire and the rest of the Greek frieze were all looking elegant and uncluttered in simple white tunics. Claire, even though she was the youngest, was the leader, and occasionally had solo steps to perform whilst the others grouped themselves about her. That morning, at the dress rehearsal, was the first time anyone had actually seen her dance. They had all been impressed, even Barge.

'I suppose she is quite *good*,' Barge had said; which coming from Barge was praise indeed.

Jo couldn't help feeling a slight tinge of resentment: she was sure that she could be as good, if only she weren't wearing this silly gauzy dress and ridiculous circlet of flowers.

She decided that what she would do was accept Melanie's uncle's advice for *part* of the time but that when it came to the dancing she would dance just as well as she knew how. That way, Miss Lintott – being a trained teacher – would see that here was a person who could rise above the mere trappings of dress. She would see that Jo was someone who simply didn't have it in her to dance badly, no matter how hard she tried. Even as she laughed at the others, she would be making mental notes to ask Claire 'who the little girl playing Peaseblossom was'.

The decision made Jo happier. She thought that she

wouldn't even mind doing a bit of squinting every now and then – the surprise when she started dancing would be all the greater.

'Everyone ready?' said Wendy, sticking her head round the door. 'I've just come to wish you good luck . . . you all look absolutely super! I just love that footwear, Margery – and is that you, Melanie, behind those teeth? Most inventive! Jo, don't forget, when you're doing your miming . . . as much mouth work as you like! The very first time you did it you had the most wonderful expression of agony on your face, and your head went from side to side. . . .' Wendy demonstrated, opening and shutting her mouth like a goldfish in a frenzy, while at the same time waving her head dramatically to and fro as if suffering acute mental anguish. Jo scowled: she didn't believe for one moment that that was how she had looked. People did exaggerate so.

'Never worry about making a fool of yourself,' said Wendy, breezily. 'Just get out there and enjoy it.'

Surprisingly, once she was on stage, Jo found that she didn't really mind so much. She even found that she was putting in little extra touches, such as flicking at the flower as it dangled over her nose, in order to make the audience laugh even more than they already were. At one point she actually heard Tom's raucous cackling. She didn't know whether Miss Lintott was amused, down in the front row, but anyway she wasn't interested in Miss Lintott being amused. What she wanted was for Miss Lintott to be impressed.

When it came to the dancing Jo simply closed her mind to Barge in her green Wellies and Melanie with her orange peel teeth and all the rest of the motley crew. She danced as she felt Claire would dance, in a world of her own.

Afterwards, there was a mad scramble to get out of their costumes and up to the gym for coffee and biscuits before it had all been pigged by everyone else. Jo especially was in a rush because of being introduced to Miss Lintott: Claire had said she might not stay after the coffee break.

Claire herself was in a different dressing room – they were using the classrooms which bordered the hall – and had already changed and disappeared by the time Jo was ready. (Tunic and sandals were much easier to get out of than net dresses with hooks and eyes all up the back.)

Wendy, in a state of excitement, met them on the stairs and told them that they had had 'more applause than anyone else' and she really thought they might be in with a chance. Jo, being totally bound up with the prospect of meeting Miss Lintott, couldn't immediately think what she was talking about. In with a chance of what? It was several seconds before she rather guiltily remembered that the whole point of the exercise was to gain points for the House.

Up in the gym, all the audience were standing about in little clusters with their cups of coffee, discussing the performances. Over in the far corner Jo could see Claire with her parents and a tall, rather stately person, with silver hair coiled into a bun, who must be Miss Lintott. Miss Lintott was talking to Lucy Abbott. A moment of jealousy pierced Jo's heart. She quelled it: her turn would come. Claire had promised. She didn't like to go over and say hallo without being invited. For one thing she wasn't sure it would be polite, and for another she had already been claimed by her own family. She would just have to be patient and wait.

'Well,' said Mrs Jameson, 'that shed a totally new light on *A Midsummer Night's Dream*, didn't it? I must say, I've always found those fairies rather tiresome!'

'Titania was good,' said Andy. 'I could go for her.'

Just for a minute, Jo took him seriously; then she realized it was his idea of a joke. She buffeted at him and said, 'What about Elizabeth Grey?'

'Which one was she?'

'She played Lysander.'

'Oh, yes! Lysander. So that was the great Liz Grey, was it?' Jo glanced round, nervously, hoping that Elizabeth wasn't in earshot. 'Yeah, I could go for her, too,' said Andy. 'No problem!'

'Know what the best bit was?' said Tom. 'Funniest bit in the whole thing?'

'No?' said Jo.

'That bit when you were dancing and that flower kept bonging up and down on your nose.' Tom gave a loud, coarse cackle. 'You didn't half look stupid!'

Jo coloured, crossly. 'I'm going to get my biscuits,' she said.

It was while she was getting the biscuits that she saw Claire and her parents, and the woman who was Miss Lintott, moving towards the door. Jo set off across the gym at a gallop. Claire surely couldn't have *forgotten*?

'Hey, Jam!' A hand shot out and snatched at her: it belonged to Matty. Jo spun round, ungraciously. What did she want?

'I just wanted to tell you,' said Matty, 'I really enjoyed it. I thought you were really good.'

'Good,' said Jo.

168

'We were all laughing,' said Matty. 'It was really funny. Specially that bit where—'

'Tell me later.' Jo shook Matty off, impatiently. 'I can't stop now!'

She had just time to register the offended expression on Matty's face before she was off again, racing full tilt after Claire across the gym.

She was almost at the door when another hand descended: this time, it belonged to Mrs Stanley.

'Jo Jameson,' she said, 'where are your manners? You have just very nearly sent that gentleman's cup of coffee flying. I think you had better go back and apologize.'

By the time Jo had apologized, and the apology had been accepted, and Mrs Stanley had read her a lecture on what she called 'hoydenish behaviour', it was too late: Miss Lintott had gone.

17

'I'm ever so sorry,' said Claire, coming up to Jo on Monday morning. 'I do feel awful.'

Jo busied herself rearranging the contents of her desk. Books *here*, pencils *there*. 'About what?' As if she didn't know. As if she hadn't spent the whole of Sunday feeling let-down and hard-done-by. But one did have one's pride to consider.

'About Miss Lintott,' said Claire. She fixed Jo earnestly with her large grey eyes. 'I completely forgot.'

'Oh, really?' Jo picked up her pencil case, unzipped it, looked inside, zipped it back up and put it away again in the same place.

'I really *meant* to introduce you,' said Claire. 'I would have done if there'd been time but she was talking to Lucy for simply ages and it just slipped my memory. But she did like the show. She said so. And she thought the elephants were really funny. She thought Barge was the funniest thing she'd ever seen. She said it was a pity Wendy couldn't have chosen just *one* trained dancer to lead you, 'cause that would have been even funnier . . . all those elephants stomping about' – Claire stomped, energetically: Jo watched, stony-faced, saying nothing – 'all big and clumsy, doing their best to imitate her . . . but it was jolly funny anyway. It was absolutely killing when you did that arabesque and started wobbling and almost kicked Barge in the face!'

'That was intentional,' said Jo. If it had happened at all. *She* couldn't remember it. A person would know if a person were wobbling, and Barge would most certainly have had something to say if Jo's foot had been anywhere near her face.

'And what about that other bit,' said Claire, 'when you turned round and went crashing into Bozzy? That was ever so funny!'

'That only happened because Bozzy was in the wrong place, and anyway I couldn't see where I was going because of that stupid flower thing squashed over my eyes.'

'Yes, but it was *funny*,' said Claire. 'All Miss Lintott was saying was that it would have been even funnier if there'd been one person doing it the right way and everyone else doing it wrong.'

'I could have done it the right way,' said Jo, angrily, 'if she hadn't made me practically *blind* having hair all in my eyes.'

'She should have had Jan doing it. She's done some ballet. She's not terribly good, but at least you can see she's had a *bit* of training.'

Jo's face grew very red. She bent over her desk, moving things methodically from one place to another.

'Anyway, said Claire, 'I am sorry. Honestly.'

Jo wished that she could be like Barge. Barge was always so gloriously pompous and crushing. She would be bound to think of something grand to say; something on the lines of, 'Pray don't worry yourself on *my* behalf. Meeting a dancing teacher is hardly to be placed in the same category as meeting the Queen, as I am sure you will agree.' The fact that she had never even set eyes on the Queen, let alone met her, wouldn't bother Barge. She was not one for troubling herself over mere details.

Jo, unfortunately, was. She had a tendency to be logical. What, after all, had the Queen to do with Claire forgetting to introduce her to Miss Lintott? Nothing at all, as far as she could see. So instead of being pompous and Bargelike and standing on her dignity, she only muttered, ''s OK. Doesn't matter,' which didn't have quite the same ring to it and certainly didn't do anything in the way of crushing.

'My memory is just so *awful*,' said Claire. 'I have to tie knots in my hanky to make sure that I remember things – unless it's something important, like an extra ballet class, or something. I wouldn't forget a thing like that. But when it's just ordinary things' – such as arranging for someone to come round to tea, or promising to introduce them to someone – 'it's terrible, really.' Claire gave a little giggle. 'My mum says I go round in a dream.'

Jo made a noise almost worthy of Barge. It sounded like 'Humph!'

'What I could do,' said Claire, 'if you like, I could get you a free ticket for our end-of-term show. Then you could come and see me dance. Would you like me to?'

Not really, thought Jo. She had lost all interest in seeing Claire dance – or in doing any dancing herself, if it came to that. If being a dancer meant forgetting promises and letting people down, then she didn't think, after all, that she would like to be one. It seemed a rather selfish sort of thing to be.

'I really ought,' said Claire, 'to make up for Saturday.'

Jo sniffed, in a Bargelike way. She hoped Claire didn't think she needed *humouring*.

'You'd enjoy it,' said Claire. 'You could come round afterwards and then I could introduce you.'

Oh, yes? She'd heard that one before. Rather noisily, Jo banged down her desk lid.

'Please don't go to any trouble on my behalf,' she said.

'Oh, it won't be any trouble,' said Claire. 'I'm entitled to four free tickets and I've only used two of them. . . .'

To everyone's extreme indignation, Sutton's and their ridiculous so-called battle scenes had won the Shakespeare competition. It was, as Barge said, completely preposterous and just went to show that the members of staff who were acting as judges knew nothing whatsoever about Shakespeare.

'Not even as if they were *proper* battle scenes . . . just a load of shrieking idiots running round in circles waving plastic swords. And did you see that armour? So obviously *card*board. Old packing cases, by the looks of things. Certainly didn't call for any acting. If it had been some kind of marching display that was required, I might have understood it. But it wasn't. They distinctly said *Shakespeare*. At least, as far as I'm aware they said Shakespeare. Of course, I may be wrong,' said Barge, ever prepared to show humility. 'I may have got hold of the wrong end of the stick. It may be that it was marching displays from the beginning and that all this time we should have been practising forming squares instead of wasting our time learning lines.'

'We did come second,' said Fij; but if that were intended as comfort it fell sadly flat. Only the glorious victory of the Nelligan senior netball team, who on Wednesday morning thrashed Sutton's into the ground, gave them any consolation in that last week of term.

173

For Jo, it was a particularly horrid sort of week. It had started badly on Sunday, when Mrs Jameson had asked her whether she still wanted ballet lessons for her Christmas present. She had gone and asked it in front of Tom, who had naturally thought it the biggest laugh of all time.

'*Ballet*?' he had cried. '*Her*?' And off he had gone, prancing round the room in hateful parody of Jo in her lopsided ballet dress with the flower dangling over her nose.

Mrs Jameson had reminded him that 'That was *supposed* to be funny. I'm sure there's no reason why Jo shouldn't dance perfectly well if she took lessons.'

'Not her!' shouted Tom. 'She's too butch. You have to be feminine to do ballet . . . like Claire.'

'Let's try and leave Claire out of this, shall we?' Mrs Jameson had turned, not unkindly, to Jo. 'You'd better let me know soon, there are only ten shopping days to go.'

Jo had said that she would think about it.

On Monday morning, for the first time ever, Matty went off to school without her. Jo waited five minutes, and when Matty didn't appear she walked up the path and knocked at the McShanes' front door. It was Matty's mum who answered it. She looked puzzled when she saw Jo. She said that Matty had left ten minutes ago . . . 'Why didn't she wait for you?'

Jo could have told her: it was because she had been horrid to Matty on Saturday night. She remembered the hurt look on Matty's face, and her own started to tingle as she walked up to the bus shop. How could she have been so beastly? Especially when Matty had only been trying to be generous and say nice things about her performance.

If I were Matty, she thought, I probably wouldn't want to talk to me any more.

It seemed that Matty didn't. She didn't purposely cut Jo dead or ignore her as they had all ignored Claire, but when Jo went up to her at break and said, 'I hope you don't think I was rude to you on Saturday' – intending to go on and explain that she hadn't *meant* to be rude – Matty just gave a loud, harsh, unMattylike sort of laugh and said, 'No, I think you've got the most charming manners!' and walked off, arms linked with Julie-Ann, before Jo could properly apologize.

At the front of 1N's classroom stood a large red pillar box made out of stiff cardboard and covered in crêpe paper. It had been put there on Monday morning by Miss Lloyd, unusually cheerful because it was almost the end of term.

'There you are,' she said. 'That's for your Christmas mail . . . last posting date is Friday morning. Delivery in the afternoon. Post now for Christmas!'

All week long people could be seen secretively pushing bundles of envelopes into it, and even, occasionally, small gift-wrapped packages. Jo and Matty traditionally exchanged presents at Christmas, but they always did it on Christmas Eve, at home. Jo didn't know whether they would this year, after what had happened on Saturday, but she had already bought Matty's present some time ago. It was a photograph album for all the photographs that she was taking with her new camera and it wouldn't have gone in the class post box in any case. She decided to send Matty a card and write 'With luv from Jam, see you Xmas Eve' inside it.

The other people she was sending cards to were Barge, Bozzy, Fij, Melanie, Nadge and Claire. The only reason she was sending one to Claire was in case no one else did. She wasn't surprised any more that people didn't like her, but she couldn't help feeling that it would be embarrassing even for Claire if she were the only person in the class not to receive a card. She might go round in a dream but she could hardly fail to notice *that*.

On Friday after lunch Gerry Stubbs, in the rôle of postman, officially opened the post box and with the help of Miss Lloyd began to sort the mail. Everyone sat watching as the piles slowly grew. Some piles grew more rapidly than others. There was one which hardly grew at all. Jo thought it was probably Claire's and felt glad, in spite of everything, that she had sent her a card. Two piles, on the other hand, quickly outstripped all the rest. One of them was bound to belong to Nadge, she was easily the most popular person in the class. The other . . . Barge, perhaps? Or people sucking up to Gerry, simply because she was form captain?

When the last item of mail had been sorted, Gerry did up each bundle in an elastic band and walked round the class delivering them. The smallest pile of all didn't go to Claire but to Lol (Jo wished, too late, that she had thought to send Lol a card. She had sent ones to the other three members of the Laing Gang; it was mean to have left out poor plump Lol). Of the two largest piles, one, predictably, went to Nadge, the other, to Jo's astonishment and disbelief, went to Claire. *Claire* – of *all* people.

Scornfully Jo turned her attention to her own (perfectly respectable) pile. How fickle people were! A fortnight ago they had all been busy sending Claire to Coventry and accusing her of anti-social behaviour; now, just because they had seen her dance and thought that one day she might become famous, they were all over her. It looked as if practically everybody in the class had sent her a card, and one or two people had even sent her presents.

Jo didn't have any presents, unless you counted a home-made calendar from Fij, but lots of people had sent her cards. Lol hadn't sent her one, so that was all right, but Naomi had, and so had Ashley and the Mouse – and she hadn't thought to send ones to any of them! Worse than that, Julie-Ann had sent her one but Matty hadn't. Getting a card from Julie-Ann made her feel bad because of all the uncharitable thoughts she kept having: *not* getting one from Matty just made her feel thoroughly miserable. It meant Matty still hadn't forgiven her for being mean.

Maybe Matty never would forgive her. I wish we could have gone to Fallowfield! thought Jo. If they had gone to Fallowfield with Trish and Laura and the rest, she and Matty might still have been friends.

Matty purposely didn't look at Jo as they left the classroom at 3.30. She knew that Jo would be going straight home, but still she didn't look at her.

Jo dawdled, unhappily, not wanting to catch Matty up and find herself waiting at the bus stop behind her and Julie-Ann.

'Jam!' It was Claire's voice calling after her. She turned, and saw Claire hurrying towards her up Shapcott Road. Once it would have pleased her to be the object of Claire's attentions: now she was unmoved.

'I nearly forgot – again!' Claire giggled, as if it were funny to keep forgetting things. Things that she had *promised*. 'Here you are. . . .' She held out an envelope.

'You've already sent me a card,' said Jo.

'This isn't a card, it's the ticket I promised you . . . it's for tomorrow afternoon, and it's in St Mary's Hall.'

'I don't know whether I'll be able to come tomorrow afternoon,' said Jo.

'But I thought you wanted to meet Miss Lintott?'

She *had* wanted to meet Miss Lintott. She really didn't care anymore.

'You ought to come,' said Claire. 'Then you could see me dance.'

The *vanity* of people! It quite took one's breath away.

'I told my mum you'd be coming. She's looking forward to meeting you again.'

Claire's mum could have met Jo last Saturday if Claire had done what she had said she would do.

'What shall I tell her?' said Claire.

'Tell her I'll come if I can,' said Jo. She would go if she felt like it. And if she didn't, she wouldn't. She didn't owe Claire anything.

On Saturday morning Jo went into town with her mother to get her hair cut. She had decided that after all it didn't suit her, having it long. Also it was more of a nuisance, especially when you were playing netball and it started to rain.

'Do I take it,' said Mrs Jameson, as they waited for the bus, 'that this means you've definitely dropped the idea of ballet lessons?'

Jo rubbed a finger up her nose. She didn't want to be accused of 'going through phases'. It was what her grandmother always said when she heard about Jo's latest enthusiasm – 'It's just a phase she's going through. It won't last.'

'I've been thinking about it,' she said. 'I've been thinking that perhaps it's rather a lot of money and you mightn't really be able to afford it.'

'One lesson a week would hardly break us!'

'No, but if I were going to do it seriously I'd need *six* lessons a week, and that would cost the earth. And if I weren't going to do it seriously,' said Jo, 'I don't think I'd really see very much point in doing it at all. Would you?'

She looked up at her mother, earnestly, through the shaggy mat of her fringe.

'I'll tell you what I think,' said Mrs Jameson. 'I think that after you've had your hair cut we ought to go and look round the shops and see if there's anything there that takes your fancy.'

There were loads of things which took Jo's fancy but nothing that she could say she really desperately wanted. She was tempted for a moment by a talking computer (which she wouldn't let Tom go anywhere *near*), and then she thought perhaps she might like an electronic organ, but she had had musical instruments before and somehow they never seemed to work for her as they did for other people, she could never get them to produce proper tunes, and the talking computer cost so much money that she would be terrified in case she lost interest and everyone would accuse her of 'going through phases' and say what a waste.

'P'raps I'll just have a new track suit,' she said. A white one, like the one Nadge had.

'We'll get you a new track suit, by all means, but I think we might be able to run to a little bit more than that . . . isn't there anything special you want?'

'Not at the moment,' said Jo. 'Maybe I'll think of something.'

They were tired after pushing round the shops in the pre-Christmas crush so Mrs Jameson said that as a treat they would go and have a coffee in one of the big stores. In fact Jo had an orange juice because of not liking coffee, and a packet of plain biscuits because of all the cakes either having cream, which made her feel sick, or horrible currants and bits of peel, but it was still a treat. Just being on her own with her mother, *without Tom*, was a treat. She said as much to Mrs Jameson, who laughed, but rather ruefully, and agreed that Tom was going through a rather tiresome phase just at the moment.

'Hopefully he'll grow out of it . . . Andy did.'

Jo couldn't remember Andy ever being quite as tiresome as Tom, though maybe that was because she had been too young at the time to notice. Confidentially, woman to woman, she said, 'I think boys *are* tiresome, don't you?'

'Oh, they have their moments,' said Mrs Jameson. 'And don't imagine you'll escape . . . when you're Tom's age you'll probably be every bit as tiresome as he is!'

'I certainly will *not*,' said Jo.

'I wouldn't take a bet on it, if I were you! What are you doing with yourself this afternoon? Going out anywhere?'

Jo wrinkled her forehead, pretending to think about it. 'I s'pose I could always go and see Claire.'

'You don't sound as if you're too keen on the idea?'

She wasn't. She had decided that being single-minded didn't make people terribly nice. She felt sorry for Mrs Kramer, worrying all the time about people not understanding how Claire's talent made it difficult for her to behave like an ordinary person, but Jo didn't see that having talent was any excuse for keeping on breaking your promises and forgetting things.

'If you don't want to see Claire,' said Mrs Jameson, 'how about Matty? You and Matty don't seem to do things together any more, these days.'

Jo frowned as she dibbled a biscuit in her orange juice, lapping it to and fro, making waves. She couldn't very well explain to her mother that she had been unbearably rude to Matty and that Matty no longer wanted to know her.

'Matty does things with Julie-Anne.'

'Who's Julie-Ann?'

'Girl in our class . . . they've got cam'ras, they go off and photograph things.'

'And that doesn't interest you?'

It wasn't that it didn't interest her – after all, you couldn't tell until you'd tried. Probably if she learnt how to do it she would find that she could take just as good pictures as anyone else. The fact was that Matty didn't *want* her. Julie-Ann had got what she had been after right from the beginning: she had got Matty to herself. Horrid scheming thing, thought Jo. She was just as mean, in her own way, as Claire. Claire had come between Tom and Nadge, Julie-Ann had come between Jo and Matty. All you could say was that Claire hadn't done it on purpose, whereas Julie-Ann had, which made her even meaner.

'Why don't you call round on the way back and see what Matty's up to?' suggested Mrs Jameson, but Jo shook her head. She knew what the answer would be.

As luck would have it, as they turned the corner into Winterbourne Avenue they saw Matty, accompanied, inevitably, by Julie-Ann, coming down the McShanes' front path.

'There!' said Mrs Jameson. She said it in tones of surprise and satisfaction, like a conjuror unexpectedly producing something out of a hat. 'There she is! Who's that with her? Is that Julie-Ann?'

Jo nodded, glumly. Matty and Julie-Ann were the last people she wanted to meet. If it hadn't been for her mother she would have turned back into the main road and gone the other way, pretending not to have seen them.

Matty and Julie-Ann came slowly up the road towards them. As usual, these days, they both had cameras slung round their necks. (Like a pair of *tourists*, thought Jo.)

'Hallo!' said Mrs Jameson. 'And how is Matty?'

Matty, who like Miles was always polite, said that she was very well, thank you.

'Glad to have broken up?' said Mrs Jameson.

Matty and Julie-Ann both solemnly chorused 'Yes.'

'So how has your first term been? Not too bad?'

'Been a lot better than I thought it was going to be,' said Matty. 'That first day, when you left us . . . I was dead scared.'

'*Were* you?' said Jo.

'Yeah, I was.'

Mrs Jameson laughed. 'You should have said! I thought you were both putting rather a brave face on things.'

I wasn't, thought Jo. I wasn't scared. Once she would have boasted about it: today, she managed to resist the temptation.

'Well, I'll leave you three to chat,' said Mrs Jameson. 'Lunch in a couple of hours, Jo. All right?'

Mrs Jameson walked on, up the road. Jo and Matty stood, awkwardly. It was Julie-Ann who spoke.

'Been Christmas shopping?' she said.

'Been to have my hair cut,' said Jo.

'It's nice like that. Suits you short. Makes your face look all pixie-ish.'

Jo knew that you ought to say thank you when people paid you a compliment – she supposed it was a compliment – but she felt too bashful. Instead, trying to show an interest, she said: 'Going anywhere special?'

'Going up the park,' said Matty, 'get some action shots.'

'Thought you were doing pavements?'

'We've done pavements. We're doing People at Play now.'

'It's for this competition.'

'We're going up the park this morning and over Crystal Palace this afternoon.'

'Want to come?' said Julie-Ann.

Jo felt her cheeks fire up. 'I haven't g-got a cam'ra. . . .'

'You could borrow your mum's.'

'It's my dad's. I don't think he'd let me.'

'She loses things,' said Matty. 'Left her purse on the bus one time.'

Julie-Ann said, 'Oh.' And then, 'In that case—'

There was a pause. Jo stood awkwardly. Matty picked at the hedge.

'S'pose there's not much point,' said Julie-Ann. 'Not if you've not got a cam'ra.'

Matty folded her piece of hedge; into one, into two, into three. Then she dug her nail through it. Without looking at Jo, she said: 'You could always come and be our model . . . sit on the swings and that.'

'*Could* I?' said Jo.

'We could do with a model,' said Julie-Ann.

'S'long as you don't mind us telling you what to do.'

'Like if we say *swing*,' said Julie-Ann.

'Or *smile*,' said Matty.

'Or *stand on your head—*'

'Or *put your arms in the air* . . . 'cause we're the photographers, see.' Matty said it earnestly, impressing upon Jo that they wouldn't be bossing her around for no reason. 'Pictures won't work if we don't set them up prop'ly. But we'll put your name on the back . . . model, Joanne Jameson.'

'You might even be *famous*,' said Julie-Ann.

'We all might be,' said Matty. 'Oh, and by the way' – awkwardly she pulled something from her pocket and thrust it at Jo – 'this is your Christmas card. I was going to push it through your door. I'm sorry I forgot to send it with the others – well, I didn't exactly for*get*,' said Matty. 'It sort of got lost. And then I found it again. I'm really sorry.'

'That's all right,' said Jo. 'I've got your present at home.'

'Yeah, me too,' said Matty.

'I'll give it you Christmas Eve.'

'Do you always give each other presents?' said Julie-Ann.

'Yes,' said Jo. 'Always.'

They turned and began walking up the road in a threesome, towards the park.

'So what are you getting from your parents? Anything special?'

'Dunno,' said Jo. 'Think I might ask for a camera. . . .'